PRAISE FOR *FIRE FIRE*

'*Fire Fire* is vibrant, fiercely intelligent and beautifully written.'
Michael Williams, *Australian Book Review*

'Slashed with its multiple flashes of refining fire and humour
both subtle and ribald, *Fire Fire* is a dark and powerful fable.'
Katherine England, *Adelaide Advertiser*

PRAISE FOR *MAHJAR*

'One cannot praise the timely grace of this book too much.'
Michael Sharkey, *The Australian*

'Sallis writes virtuoso prose which on the surface is deceptively
simple, but is remarkable in its psychologically penetrating
breadth.' David Wood, *Canberra Times*

'Superb stories, astonishing in their range and power; subtle,
brave, unbearably moving.' Helen Garner

'Sallis wields her great gifts of empathy and eloquence to
render human beings in full, unflinching detail. It is a book of
journeys, passionate and powerful.' Geraldine Brooks

PRAISE FOR *THE CITY OF SEALIONS*

'A rich book — a lyrical account of a girl's growth and self-
discovery, and at the same time a deeply sympathetic
exploration of Muslim culture.' J.M. Coetzee

PRAISE FOR *HIAM*

'A debut that is truly stunning.'
Australian Bookseller and Publisher

'Its brilliance, innovation and daring is undeniable.'
Australian Book Review

ALSO BY EVA SALLIS

Fiction

Hiam (1998)
The City of Sealions (2002)
Mahjar (2003)
Fire Fire (2004)

Non-fiction

Sheherazade through the Looking Glass:
The Metamorphosis of the 1001 Nights (1999)

Co-edited anthologies

with Brenda Glover, Kim Mann and Scott Hopkins
Painted Words (1999)
with Rebekah Clarkson, Kerrie Harrison, Gabrielle
Hudson, Lisa Jedynak and Samantha Schulz
Forked Tongues (2002)
with Heather Millar and Sonja Dechian
Dark Dreams: Australian Refugee Stories by Young Writers
11–20 Years (2004)

the Marsh Birds

EVA SALLIS

ALLEN&UNWIN

First published in 2005 5/07

Copyright © Eva Sallis 2005

This project has been assisted by the Commonwealth
Government through the Australia Council, its arts
funding and advisory board.

Australia Council
for the Arts

Allen & Unwin
83 Alexander Street
Crows Nest NSW 2065
Australia
Phone: (61 2) 8425 0100
Fax: (61 2) 9906 2218
Email: info@allenandunwin.com
Web: www.allenandunwin.com

National Library of Australia
Cataloguing-in-Publication entry:

Sallis, Eva.
    The marsh birds.

    ISBN 1 74114 600 3.

    1. Refugees—Australia—Fiction. I. Title.

A823.3

Set in 12/15 pt Bembo by Asset Typesetting Pty Ltd
Printed in Australia by McPherson's Printing Group

10 9 8 7 6 5 4 3 2 1

For the boys I love, especially Roger and Rafael

1

*D*hurgham's chest hurt. His heart hammered in its bed of pain. It was the third day and all his limbs ached. He had sat on this same block of stone near the main entrance of the mosque, night and day, huddled just enough out of sight to deflect attention, just enough in sight for his mother to see him, instantly, to run to him and cup his face … and then, and then!—it would all be over. His father would wrap his arms around him and squeeze so tight that all the pain left him. He gasped his tears back at the expectancy of it. Now! Now! Right now, they would come around that corner or out of the shadows of the Souq al Hamidiya, hesitant under the broken arch, then breaking into a run. He could see the anger of relief after worry, now! Now!

If we get separated, we meet together at the Great Mosque.

If we get separated—

3

He had slunk around the mosque, expectant and with his heart hammering, always hammering. Three days! He stuck close to the wall. The mosque was the only certain thing.

We meet together at the Great Mosque.

Sometimes he even kept his hands on the corner stones, as if touch more than sight could confirm he had done the right thing. He was certain his father had said the Great Mosque and that in all the world there was no other. This was the greatest, oldest mosque. He knew that, even from school.

He couldn't leave it further than a few steps. After the first three days, he slept in the broken garden near the tomb of Salahuddin, curled up in the darkness against the ancient mosque wall. At night he was afraid. He made himself small against the cold stone, his heart pounding him into the ground, and with the dawn prayers he was on his block of stone again. He could feel his heart breaking.

He couldn't bring himself to go inside. The crowds flowed by him with the adhan and then by him again at the end of prayers. If anyone greeted him, nodded to him to come inside too, Dhurgham answered shyly that he had to wait for his parents. But people mostly ignored him or didn't see him at all.

Occasionally other small boys about his age or younger played in the cobbled square between the mosque and the crumbling entrance to the Souq al Hamidiya. They called out to him a few times, raucously—who was he, what was his father's name, where from, then to come and join them, but to each question he shook his head, suddenly too shy, too alone, to find words. They had funny accents and giggled at him when he spoke. They kicked their soccer ball at him to provoke him into participation, but when the ball struck him and rolled off and away, they gave up. They shouted a few insults at him, shook their heads at him in mimicry, then left him alone.

After that, now and then, he wanted to play. A kind of certainty about the world restored him and his spirits rose. His parents couldn't be that far away. He was going to feel really silly for all his fears when they showed up. He was the first to make it to Damascus, that was all. *I won!* he'd crow to Nooni, and she'd punch him, narrow her eyes at him. And then, when she found out that he'd been a bit scared, she'd say, *You big silly*, and shove him this way and that. The only thing that stopped him playing then was the thought of them catching him being carefree when the situation called for more sedate adult behaviour. There was the money sewn into his blazer to think of. Not a good idea to fold his blazer neatly on the ground and keep an eye on it. To play he would have to hug it close to his body with his hands in his pockets. He would look silly.

On the morning of the fifth day, he thought suddenly that as long as he was in or around the mosque, they would find him. He didn't need to wait at the al Hamidiya entrance. They would go everywhere, they would look for him. He smiled to himself, very pleased. He was clever to guess it. He was certain he was right. He could feel his mother's anxiety, how feverishly she would hunt for him in every possible corner, inside and out, even in the streets around the mosque, even if she herself had to stay there day and night. She was born in Syria, he thought— near the border with Iraq, but nonetheless in this same country. He touched the Syrian stones with a new familiarity and was immensely cheered. She would use her Syrian voice, her knowledge of everything Syrian. Everyone would respect and obey her. He felt a light lift to his step and walked again the three quarters way round the mosque and back. He didn't dare go all the way round because the souq and alleys seemed to come right up against the mosque at one point, and he felt himself leaving it behind if he headed around them to find the route back to the other side of the great walls. He really had a lot of space that was safe. And of course there was inside. All safe—a huge realm.

He went round to the side by the garden in which he slept and for the first time turned his back on the possible roads by which his father, mother and sister would arrive (any minute now). He walked in through the great open door. He was sure no one would stop him, even though Damascus was strange in lots of ways. Just inside, he removed his shoes.

The mosque was huge inside, far bigger than its outer perimeter made it seem. It was unbelievably quiet, given the noise outside. Students were reading here and there in the shade of the great arcades that ran to the left and the right, seated on the marble floor that spread like a still lake across to the other side. He felt strangely free. He padded softly along the arcade to the left. He sought out a space free of people and sat down himself on the cool marble. Here he found he could imagine his mother finding him, his father's austere relief, Nura's delight as if these were already events of the long distant past, events remembered with pain and pleasure but with no urgency or terror or doubt. It was nothing really. The mosque was ancient and had seen far greater tragedies and troubles. He could remember some of them from his schoolbooks and beguiled himself for hours with that connection anyone can feel when touching and seeing a place that brings the past into the present.

It was more. The mosque seemed to be able to be in the future as much as the past and to swallow the pain of the present. He stayed almost all day in that vast expanse of marble calm and shade.

He felt very pleased for a while. He prayed too when the adhan rang out and the great hall of pillars on the far side filled with rustling, sniffing, coughing, sweating people. He flowed in with them, washed and knelt with them on the carpet. He flowed out again into the marble expanse as if that great monument were living, breathing them all in and out in huge, measured breaths.

Then he remembered Ali and his panic slowly welled back up like a returning tide. It drove him back outside into the noisy now of the city, to his step across from the ancient souq.

When his certainty ebbed away, it was usually with the memory of the man called Ali and his strange kiss.

First the van, and men holding him, not unkindly, and his voice screaming in the darkness, drowning the distant dulled natter of automatic fire. 'Stop Stop Stop, Wait Wait W-w-w-wait a little bit!' His voice breaking into a scream and their voices coming from here and there in the fear-filled muttering darkness. 'No. Go!— No headlights!' Dhurgham screamed and cried and shook the van with all his strength. He even bit the man holding him. A hairy face came up close to him in the darkness. 'Sorry, habibi,' a cool voice said, and he felt the swoosh of something through the air behind his head but not the impact.

He was under carpet, its fibres on his face and the heavy wool smell in his nostrils. He half heard words in the darkness—*with only the boy, and him asleep under the rug, no need*. He drifted down and away again.

He came to in daylight with a terrible headache. There were three men in the van. The man who had spoken to him in the dark caught his eye and said, 'Good morning, ya Ibni. I'm Ali. Don't talk. Your family will follow if they can.' The men were tight-lipped but kind. They sounded like Syrians, or at least not like

Iraqis. Dhurgham huddled in the van, thinking, trying to remember all that had happened. They were already in Syria, Ali said.

The journey was long, hot, unremarkable. He felt as though his body had been left behind, as though he was still in the dim marshes, and this daylight and interminable vibration were a strange dream. He couldn't think clearly and he had too much to think about to pay the road any attention. Then the anxiety grew on him that it was up to him to pay them. He sidled up to Ali and tried to whisper in the most manly way he could about the amount. 'It's all sorted by your father, habibi,' Ali said, and Dhurgham felt inordinately comforted.

They drove into Damascus in a fug of tension. Dhurgham stared out of the window at the teeming foreign city, his mind numb. He realised dully that he was a very long way from home.

They dropped Dhurgham on the street at a place they called a 'safe house'. Ali got out with him and pressed a small wad of Syrian money into his hands. Dhurgham was too surprised and shy to say anything, although he knew he should have protested to be polite. Then Ali kissed him on the forehead, holding Dhurgham's head for two long seconds against his lips, and leapt back behind the wheel. Then they sped away and that was the last time he saw them or their van.

Dhurgham looked at the shuttered windows and high walls of the safe house.

He didn't hesitate. He turned and caught the first passing taxi to the Great Mosque.

Dhurgham knew he was the littlest and liked it. In his family, this made him all-powerful. He didn't know that he didn't know much. He didn't think much about his mother's moods, her asthma, or his father's work, absences, worries. Had he thought about it, he would have said that he liked his father to have worries. He himself had none, not yet, and his father having them meant that his father was doing all the necessary things. Dhurgham would have been concerned if his father had suddenly appeared worry-free, as if that might reveal a lessening of his father's status and responsibilities. He loved Ahmad, the other adult male in their household, in fact spent far more time with Ahmad than he did with his father; but, as Ahmad had far fewer and much less mysterious worries, he was clearly less involved in the troubles of maintaining the world than his father. Ahmad was their part-time caretaker, doorman and handyman.

Dhurgham's favourite place as a little boy was Ahmad's narjeela-repair workshop out the back of the café Hassan Ajmi on al Mutanabbi Street in old Baghdad. Everyone needed narjeela repairs but not many paid for them. For a while Ahmad got chickens in payment from his regulars, then copper wire, eggs, car radiators and miscellaneous junk that began to pile up around their house and disappear as theft became widespread. Ahmad never refused anything he was offered, even when an Ishtar freezer and a troop-carrier chassis joined the junk filling the street. 'People need a smoke,' he said. 'Even if there is no proper tobacco.' But Hassan Ajmi was always crowded: their tobacco was excellent. It came, via a complicated series of trans-actions, from the son of the President.

Ahmad hadn't always worked in a narjeela-repair workshop. Dhurgham's father said it was a hobby. But from the first year of the embargo, Ahmad had become known as the best hubble-bubble repairer in Baghdad. The shop was a small alcove squeezed at the back of the café and partly jutting into the neighbouring book-shop. The workshop had a rug, a gas burner with a bright blue flame, a coffee pot, tools, resin and wax spots and lumps scattered about. The shelves in the darkness were packed with disassembled pipes, stems, bowls and stands, and the walls were hung with the polished and finished pieces, waiting, sometimes for months, to be collected. Early in the war, when adults were still shocked to inaction and children still charm-ed by the changes around them, the spice souq some streets over was hit by a stray missile, missing al Mutanabbi Street but flattening the spices with what was to be the sweetest smelling bomb of the war. 'Following its nose,' Uncle Mahmoud said, imitating a missile. This had left an open space that soon became a shanty souq and a thieves' market with surprising supplies. Ahmad managed to get all he needed somehow.

The hot resin smells rising from the dish on the burner, the smell of beeswax against the polished coconut bowl, the scent of lemon brass polish, the smell of coffee and sweet moist tobacco, and the smell of Ahmad's deft fingers slightly singed: these were the smells of Dhurgham's kingdom when he was very small. He himself had a special spot, a red Turkoman rug on a box to the left of the burner, and, sitting there, he thought the men who frequented the café to smoke and chat would see that he was lordly, that he owned this, his domain and, to a certain degree, theirs. He answered them with his deepest voice in measured phrases, no abbreviations, when they called greetings to him, but he hated it when they smiled and called him a little prince, turning him into a little boy who should sit still while Ahmad worked. At other times, Ahmad gave him a sweet-smelling rag and let him polish the burnished coconut bowls of the finest pieces, and he sat there proud, the worker, doing real work.

The workshop was both palace-like and cave-like: glittering layers in the darkness—brown bowls, scrolled brass, ornate cut tin and wood necks and plush velvet hoses and silver worked mouthpieces—all, except for the ones he polished, covered in dust. He loved the feel of the hot wax on his finger and the crisp cap it formed on his fingertip when it cooled. He loved the smell of the apple tobacco Ahmad sucked from an ancient narjeela and breathed in gentle curlicues from his nostrils. And he loved Ahmad's narjeela. It had horses and riders, European knights and Bedu warriors fighting in the gold and silver base and crown of the bowl, and it had three swords for feet. The long pipe was old and worn, mangy even, like an old dog, but the mouthpiece was ebony inlaid with pure silver. When he was very young, he had wished his father had a hubble-bubble like this one, and that his father did something as manly as smoke it in a narjeela-repair workshop. One day he said as much to Ahmad, who gave him a look and said, 'Your daddy is the one on this horse, Dhurgham, not the one smoking the pipe.' And he touched a singed finger to the leading warrior, who was standing high in his stirrups. Dhurgham tingled with a sudden anxiety and pride. Then he swung his legs and secretly revelled in the vast universe of troubles that his father kept at bay, leaving him, Dhurgham, free altogether, and Ahmad only frowning slightly over a glowing burner.

His father's body, whether on the horse on the narjeela, or seated with a sinewy forearm draped over a raised knee, was both warmth and distance, both the tight embrace and the far perimeter of Dhurgham's world. That thrumming body was as permanent to him as the arch of stars at night and spanned his world with the same certainty and grandeur.

On the eighth day, instead of straining to see each new person, he shut his eyes, thinking, *They will see me, regardless.* And he felt their eager desire, their longing for him, their eyes reaching through the spangled air for his sweet familiar form, for *him*. Whenever he shut his eyes, the world sped up, urgent with pain and reunions. He tried imagining them approaching, he unaware; then he would fling his eyes open, ready to be startled, to sob a little to please his mother, to struggle a little bit in her embrace, to hold his sobs back to impress his father. He sobbed into his sleeve without control at that and his eyes opened.

The world slowed to normal. They were never there among the flapping desperate footsteps that he could hear with his eyes closed.

Once, with his eyes shut, he drifted away from the false patter of feet approaching that never came near and found himself thinking of his yellow and red truck. He had not had batteries for it for most of his life, since before the war, but it was nonetheless his favourite. He saw it on the top step by the bathroom, on the landing leading to his and Nooni's rooms. He could see the darkened doorway to Nooni's. His door was shut because he had left a mess tumbled about in there. He had been delighted when his mother said, *Just leave everything as it is.* Not even his bed was made. He could see that little kid's mess, his clothes, his Pokémons, his old Winnie Dubdoub, his Spiderman poster; and the truck, alone in the empty house *for days now, nearly two weeks.* Ahmad wouldn't even have put it away, because when they locked up, Ahmad wasn't there, and his uncle had said that Ahmad had gone home to his village for good. No one was there. It was empty, silent, just the yellow and red truck and his mess and Nooni's dark room. He began to cry again, his head down in the crook of his elbow.

'Who will fill the tank, Nooni, if Ahmad is gone?'

'You will, silly. Build up your strength. A hundred buckets should take you five minutes!'

'Who will look after the orchard?'

'You!'

'Who will sweep?'

Nura tapped him in the chest with a forefinger.

Ahmad leaving was the most serious thing that had happened since the end of the war. He said as much to Nura, who laughed at him.

'What, more serious than your mum becoming an egg seller? More serious than the poor people *dying*?' Nura lowered her voice so their mother wouldn't hear, 'More serious than going to hospital to visit Uncle Mahmoud?'

Dhurgham shuddered but he wanted to make a point. This was the first time the embargo had really affected his everyday life.

It wasn't the embargo at all. Three days later, they left in the middle of the night.

Sometime on the ninth day, he went numb. The sun was slanting down across the cobbled stones. The street was deserted, the mosque full for prayers. He stayed outside, unable this time to tear himself from his vigil, not for hope, but for the weight of his despair. The sunlight had a cruel silence. The sunlight was as empty as darkness. The world was empty. Nura and his father and mother were not in it. The expectancy leaked out and the pain constricting his throat and rib cage stiffened, setting in his brittle body; a pain hooped and frozen.

He sat without hope, then, day after long day, aching, barely able to get the energy to buy maarouk, barely chewing to eat it. Ammar the maarouk seller was nice. He wheeled the cart over to Dhurgham whenever he saw him. He smiled and said hello in his funny Syrian way. Dhurgham liked the sort with dates and sesame but mostly forced himself to buy the plain.

Just ten lira each. Ammar laughed a lot and one day gave Dhurgham a cigarette to smoke. Dhurgham kept it in his top pocket.

Maarouk, to keep soldiers on their feet, he thought. Eating maarouk he wasn't spending very much. He hadn't touched the money in his coat. The Syrian money Ali had given him would last at least another three weeks. They would think he had done well, looking after it all so carefully! But there was no glimmer in his heart. They were gone.

It was a terrible six days.

Dhurgham knew that he was the darling. Nura knew it too and teased him for being spoilt.

'You'll never get anywhere without me and Mum right there beside you to do everything for you.'

'You'll see, Nooni. I'm going to be a scholar and a pilot. I'm going to be a diplomat. A general. A very diplomatic general. The first man to bring peace to Palestine. I'm like Sayf bin dhi Yazan—it is meant to be. If you want to help me do such things, you can,' he said with expansive generosity.

'The first man to get a sesame cookie, more like.' Nura sneered. '"You'll grow strong if you eat, eat, eat, apple of my eye."'

He was undaunted. 'Don't worry, Nooni, it won't

17

be one-way traffic. I'll even smack your husband one if he needs it.'

Nura slapped him in the chest and raised her eyebrows at him. 'Shhhh, silly. I'm not getting married.' Then she smiled and squeezed him tight.

He grinned. He was her favourite too. Nura hated everybody else these days. The angrier she got, the more pleased Dhurgham became: he increasingly got his witty, feisty sister all to himself.

Sometime around the fifteenth day, his hope returned. His father was so strong! His mother so strict and stern. Nura so funny! They were captured, he thought. Tortured. But now, resourceful and beloved even of his captors, his father was in the process of escaping. His father would come and get him; then they would together rescue the others: Nura first, then his mother, then his uncle, aunt and cousins. The explanations began to parade through his mind and he smiled to himself. His mother would be cross to feel these ribs poking out! He had better feed himself a bit to please her. He giggled. How delicious it would be to be scolded! He was strong, too, like his father. No more of these tears! He had so often said, 'I am strong, aren't I, Mummy, for a twelve year old!' His mother would sometimes say *yes*, exasperated; but on rare occasions she would smile, stop what she was doing, and look closely, her face lit up with wonder at his extraordinary physical, moral and spiritual strength.

He imagined anything to keep himself from touching the emptiness of those six days. He began to imagine that every person who eyed him with more than a cursory glance was a messenger.

He became, in no time at all, a hollow-cheeked blank-eyed child, smiling now and then to himself, muttering sometimes. A small dot at the heart of an old city that is itself built over countless layers of past lives, countless buried cities. There are and have been thousands of such children in this city, any city; odd fruit, there to be picked or to wither away. Curled up in filthy clothes, familiar but unknown around the mosque. He could have stayed for the rest of his life, inscribed into the ordinary day by the repetition of the tiny marks of his presence, provided he did nothing that could really distinguish him from the inanimate steps and broken stone.

He lived in a kind of darkness, feeling his way around the mosque, touching the same spot on the same stones in an endlessly repeated ritual, counting the steps from one point to the next, regulating in muttered seconds and minutes the time he rested between stepping out the same circuit, pacing himself until he could allow himself his rationed time inside.

The call to prayer structured his day. His active duty outside and his stillness within. He knew the mosque so well, inside and out, that he made his way around as a blind boy might have. But his time inside the mosque was illuminated by a form of dark ecstasy that depended on his eyes. In that vast expanse of peace and coolness he found his own pain mattered little. His waiting had adopted its strict pattern. He would wash his hands and face and neck and pray in the great prayer hall, numbed and charmed. Then, in the huge open courtyard, he would sit and lean back against the wall of the arcade between two pillars, regulating his place by moving one pillar along each day, furious and disoriented if someone was already in his chosen spot, unsettled and uncertain as his slow orbit was disrupted by the pillars of the entrance and the carpeted prayer hall. He was framed, held up as he slumped, in massive glory. He studied the mosaics, letting every leaf, every faceted building, every perfect fruit, every motionless wave be imprinted in its leaping stillness onto his mind.

His field of vision each day allowed him one piece of an evolving whole. It took him sixty-three days to make his way all the way around the mosque. When he began a new circuit he laughed quietly as he found wholly new things to see in the familiar images. He began to imagine that, behind the unchanging windows of one exquisite heavenly tower in the mosaics, an eternal boy looked out at him, missing him when something obscured the line of vision. His best days were when the eternal boy could see him. His winter was the long sequence under the southern arcade, which passed under the wall on which the boy's tower was depicted. He passed these twenty three days slowly, waiting for his spring when he would turn the corner into the easterly arcade and see from that oblique angle a gold line that was the tower.

He found that he could live, day after day, waiting for them, but his memory stopped working. He could not remember the marshes. The van was a fact that made him want to go to the toilet, but he couldn't remember anything in it and he avoided looking at vans or thinking of the word. He could not remember why exactly he waited on those stone blocks, what was delaying them. He knew their faces and held them close. He knew words only: Baghdad. Marshes. Van. His mind was a fuzzy blank, as if tuned out.

'As-salaam aleykum.'

'Waleykum as-salaam.'

'What are you doing, son?'

'Waiting.'

Three times Mr Hosni asked and three times got the same answer.

The fourth time, Dhurgham greeted him first.

The fifth time, Mr Hosni was inspired.

'Hey,' he said in a low voice. 'Come with me now, quickly, quickly. I know where they are.'

Dhurgham's eyes shone, suddenly, richly, and Mr Hosni jumped with the pleasant shock of it.

'My parents?' the boy breathed.

'Maybe,' Mr Hosni said, glancing to the left and the right in arch secretiveness. 'Come, now!'

Dhurgham leapt up and grasped the extended hand.

'What about my sister?' he whispered, beaming, breathless with the terror that it was a dream.

'There there,' Mr Hosni said awkwardly, stroking the boy's head. He put his arm around the thin shoulders, seeking through his register for something motherly. Dhurgham began to sob, softly at first, then in deep, sawing grief, bitten deeper with each breath. Mr Hosni cuddled him close, bent over him, crooning in a gentle falsetto. The two rocked stiffly side by side, Dhurgham threshing with his grief until he fell asleep in Mr Hosni's lap. Mr Hosni stopped crooning and looked down speculatively at the boy. Would clean up OK, maybe. Too thin, for now. He lifted Dhurgham slowly and carried him upstairs.

The child was so heavy!

But when he undressed Dhurgham he found it was the filthy clothes that were heavy.

'Sleep, little bird,' he said in wonder, smiling. 'Baba Hosni is here now,' and, surprised by feeling genuinely solicitous, he tucked the blanket tight around the thin body. He was such a pretty boy, too. And alone with all that money for so long! It must have been meant to be.

When Dhurgham awoke, he was naked under a soft clean blanket, in a bed for the first time in months. His body shuddered and then settled into the giant relief that rose up through him from his toes to his ears. He kept his eyes shut, blissful, half asleep. 'Nura?' he said, but there was no answer. He could smell something that made it all wrong and he stiffened. He didn't call out again. He buried his head under the blanket and realised that the smell was himself. He stank terribly. He opened his eyes and clutched his own chest, his fingers splayed in the dim purple light under the bedclothes, and the shock of his boniness, the grid of his ribs, shot through him. He leapt up. His clothes were nowhere to be seen. He was in a strange airy room with an open door. He raced down the stairs stark naked, furious, roaring the way his father would have but feeling like crying. He knew he was small and thin and couldn't use his own name.

Mr Hosni was a smart man. He told himself that he would get to the bottom of the money business, then, if it really was the boy's, he would invest it, taking just board and keep, just board and keep. He had been up since the break of day, not for prayers, oh no. He had first thought of just disappearing, leaving the boy to make his own way, destitute, into the darkness that swallows such children, but he was too curious. Too many stories had delivered such misleadingly dressed boys only to follow with much more, much more. And not just fantasy stories either, especially these days. The boy was almost certainly Iraqi. Who was he? What if he, Hani Hosni, Mr Soft and Sweet, became the saviour of a genuinely valuable kid?

He was decided. He laid the money out in piles on the table and put the clothes in the bin. He knew that when the boy came screaming down the stairs in the morning to accuse, the money had to be out in the open, or they'd never get off on the right foot. It would tell him in an instant, too, whether the boy was a thief or a rich kid. A rich kid would be relieved to have an older man help him look after the money. *A thief*, Mr Hosni told himself happily, *won't hear of it and can be turfed straight out the door.* So when Dhurgham announced himself with an escalating rage down the stairs and erupted into the room, Mr Hosni couldn't help smiling broadly. Naked! Just like that! Only one of those little princes would do that! He didn't even need to scrutinise that face for its relief or fear at the sight of the neat piles.

• • •

Mr Hosni's apartment was upstairs above a carpet shop just off al Hariqa Square in the old city, minutes from the Souq al Hamidiya. It was a flaking, chipped and rusted apartment of two floors at the top of one of the newer older buildings. The street was lined with similar buildings, streetside shops and above them offices; indeed Mr Hosni's spacious apartment was made up out of part of the upper floor of an office and a mulhaq, a small courtyard apartment on the roof, designed originally for keeping life and work close together. It was nice inside—well furnished and tasteful. Mr Hosni lived there alone, revelling in his space. He was a fastidious and thrifty man who nonetheless liked fine things and small luxuries when he could afford them. His apartment and his tastes were oddly genteel. They revealed someone who had once lived with wealth and regarded it with sentimentality and nostalgia, as something that could be evoked by this or that object, or a particular arrangement of furniture and old-fashioned decor. He did his own cooking, cleaning, washing, plumbing and motorbike repairs, and, as he could do anything he set his hands to, despised experts and professionals. He kept the apartment clean and pleasant. He insisted Dhurgham clean his own room.

Dhurgham's room was the nicest room on the top floor. It was light and open, looking out both over the street and into the courtyard, which was the rooftop. There were two other rooms on that floor, usually locked. Mr Hosni repaired small electronic toys and

25

digicams in one and had a computer, scanner, DVD burner and photo albums in the other. Work and leisure, he called these two rooms. Dhurgham's room had good furniture of pale gold wood, plain but with subtle style in its rounded and bevelled edges. Mr Hosni bought him a new mattress the week he arrived. He had a white bedspread over clean linen, washed weekly and dried in the sun on the rooftop. The soap powder Mr Hosni used smelt of his early childhood and Dhurgham had torn and troubled dreams in the fug of his own body and those sun-crisped Bonix-fresh sheets.

Dhurgham settled in immediately, suddenly numb. Leaving the mosque and washing the dirt from his body had a strange effect. From the first day, he stopped muttering and reciting and appeared like a normal boy. He stayed attuned to the call to prayer, held by it to the faint thread of his story; but he found he could not pray. Prayer itself seemed utterly bound with the mosque and with his grief. Whenever the adhan rang out he felt a strange mix of heightened anxiety and intense relief, and he often cried as everyone would have been praying. The severance from his other rituals caused him little pain.

He worried that he should be waiting at the mosque but he made no move at first to go back there. After a few days he began to yearn for the mosque as though he had lost a kind of bliss; yet he knew he had never felt anything like happiness there. The shadows and glories flitting through his mind had no tangible resemblance to what he could remember and he did nothing. Indeed, going there also seemed unbearable. The minaret and tower could be seen from his window. He kept his curtains drawn enough to cover them.

It was as though paying board to Mr Hosni (*You are a man now*, Mr Hosni had said), yet letting Mr Hosni look after everything, the money, the food, and his comings and goings, settled something and made him lose all but a fantasy of hope. He would lie awake at night, thinking that Nura and his mother and father were angry with him but sensing something very bad underneath it all that his mind wouldn't touch. A blanket or mist descended on him if he tried to think back further than the mosque. He had almost chosen his forgetfulness while he was waiting by the mosque; but now, when he tried, he found he could not choose to return. His past was taken from him. Occasionally when half asleep he would hear a voice but not what it said, and he would hover, not over his white bed, but as if taking a bird's view of a marsh, looking down in the dim fog-streaked starlight. He would almost feel the rub of heavy swinging clothes. He would sweat and shake, yet all he saw was unbearably beautiful.

After a couple of weeks he forced himself to go to the Great Mosque a few times with Mr Hosni but was so overwhelmed each time that he was physically ill, and Mr Hosni convinced him gently not to go again, saying that when his parents came for him, they would know that the rendezvous was stale and would try other means. Mr Hosni said he knew people who knew people who knew people and if his little bird's parents appeared anywhere in Damascus, he'd hear of it within a week. Dhurgham believed him but still hung onto the days in grief and homesickness.

Mr Hosni explained each expense and stacked the money on the table often in order to show Dhurgham what it took to clothe and feed and house him, what it took to pay the doctor for sleeping tablets and antidepressants, and what it took to pay his scouts who were scouring the city for Dhurgham's parents. Dhurgham, who had never thought of his family's resources, saw the slow shortening of the stacks and the disappearance of the jewellery as the ebbing away of all certainty. When the money was gone, a long time in the future but also inevitable, then his family would have nothing; he would both have lost them, leaving them with nothing, and used up all they had. He wondered what they would think and whether his mother would be angry with him for his mismanagement, whether he should be spending any of it. Mr Hosni pointed out that he would starve if he didn't and they wouldn't want that, and for that Dhurgham had no answer. Dhurgham got completely sick of the sight of it and he was relieved when Mr Hosni, seeming to sense his misery, stopped showing or talking about the money.

Mr Hosni stopped seeing his circle of friends. He stopped fiddling with electronics or staying in his leisure room until late in the night. Looking after the boy became his project. He bought different foods, cooked meals once or twice a day and took Dhurgham to the doctor to get advice and prescriptions, then to the chemist for tablets. He felt a warm glow when the doctor said, 'Your nephew is a lucky boy that he had you to adopt him.' He regarded himself with some wonder at the end of each happy day. Was this all it took? Why hadn't he picked one up before? In the market he would look at the street boys, but their loud voices, their confidence, their jaunty or broken bodies, their plainness when they looked crushed, filled him with disgust. None of them measured up to his Birdie. He could find no boy that, now he had his sweet sad boy at home, might have tempted him. Then he thought to himself that it was because Dhurgham was sad. These boys looked too brash, too happy; and in any case there was no knowing whether they had parents, brothers and sisters, just like any other impoverished kid who looked abandoned as a strategy.

He took Dhurgham shopping for clothes each time he remembered yet another item that a child might need. He took great pleasure in it. Dhurgham accompanied him, large-eyed and silent, and said nothing at all when Mr Hosni said, 'My Nephew' to every shopkeeper. Mr Hosni bought singlets and three pairs of pyjamas. He bought underpants in several different colours. He bought T-shirts for casual around the house and good shirts for out. His nephew was not going to look like any street urchin. His nephew would show them. When Dhurgham accompanied him in a stylish striped and embroidered shirt and pressed tan trousers, Mr Hosni swelled with pride. He wondered occasionally to himself whether his passion for caring for the boy would wear off and the novelty of playing parent fade, but it didn't. Dhurgham remained just dependent enough and just aloof enough to be charming and mysterious. Mr Hosni found himself planning for a future together.

He didn't want Dhurgham to go to school. School would fill the boy with ideas. School would take Birdie away for six hours of every day. School scared Mr Hosni. At school, the boy would make friends, get cheeky, learn to despise a benefactor. School would fill his lovely little head with things that had nothing to do with the real world. He was delighted to find that the boy was thoroughly literate. That was all it took to live in full enjoyment of the world. He would teach the boy the rest himself. He'd teach him the ways of the world, freed from the swindle of schools and teachers. He'd teach him that a body is nothing to be ashamed of. He'd teach him all there was to know about computers. And as soon as he thought of it, he raced out and bought Dhurgham his own computer, with a slightly second-hand Pentium II. When the boy blushed a fierce red and muttered something about the money, Mr Hosni said, 'No No No, Birdie, this one's on me. This one's your birthday present. Your old Uncle is going to give you an education.' Dhurgham sat down and began weeping. Mr Hosni hugged him and upped his Prozac dose.

Mr Hosni went to bed blissful. He had never felt so whole, so healed and open of heart.

Mr Hosni sang tunefully as he cooked breakfast. One morning Dhurgham sang with him and they smiled to each other over their tomato, zaater, khubz and labne.

As a young boy Dhurgham had always thought west-erners cultured. People of privilege, peace and progress. The only westerners he had met had been diplomats and United Nations people and a Finnish film-maker his father had entertained at their house. His father's stories from his university days in London had been stories of admiration and appreciation. His father's anger at America or the United Nations was not directed at Americans. But with Mr Hosni, Dhurgham began to see westerners as predators. Mr Hosni was intensely conscious of westerners and would whisper about them whenever he saw tourists of any kind. Every time they went out to a coffee shop or restaur-ant, Mr Hosni would lean in close, his eyes flicking back and forth over the tables and passers-by, and murmur or even whisper a stream of speculation and revelations. Dhurgham would get a run-down on the dress, class and sexual behaviour of the westerners who sat and smoked or walked past. Mr Hosni also knew many of them and knew terrible things about them. Some of them knew him and came over to say hello, and Mr Hosni would behave deferentially and courteously but then tell stories of rape and depravity that made Dhurgham look again at these clean-shaven figures and have nightmares.

Mr Hosni loved people-watching. These excursions into gossip and the frightening world beneath people's façades became a feature of their life together. Mr Hosni, who was himself afraid of people, felt immeasurably strengthened by having someone to whom he could tell all the terrible secrets that had crept into his range of vision. Mr Hosni never forgot anything. The only people Mr Hosni feared and hated more than westerners were the police.

Mr Hosni called off the scouts seeking Mr and Mrs Nasr and their daughter, lost somewhere without money in Damascus. Dhurgham writhed in horror at night, wondering whether his parents had guessed what he had named himself and them; sure, almost sure, that Nura would guess. He could hear his father's voice over and over: *Once we cross the border, never use our real name. We'll get new identity papers as soon as we get to Damascus.* He couldn't bring himself to confide in Mr Hosni. He knew Mr Hosni had guessed from the start

32

that he was lying about his name, for he was an inexperienced liar. He was bewildered by the satisfaction that gleamed from his benefactor at the lie.

'Birdie by name, Birdie by nature!' Mr Hosni would croon sometimes. Other times he would murmur, 'My little Eagle will fly, ooh yes. One of these days.'

Dhurgham began to hate the name. *Never use our real name. NEVER use our real name.*

'Your body is nothing to be ashamed of,' Mr Hosni sang softly as he soaped Dhurgham's legs and thighs. Dhurgham stood passively in the basin. 'It is a most beautiful body, too, Birdie, and you should be proud. With a body like yours you should never be unhappy.'

Mr Hosni sighed as he began to soap Dhurgham's belly and chest in gentle sweeping movements. He looked up and noticed that Dhurgham was crying softly and Mr Hosni felt tears start in his own eyes. He patted Dhurgham's head with his foamy mitten, leaving a huge dollop in his hair.

'Don't cry, Birdie! Your life will be much happier and much better than mine—trust me on that! I'll take care of you and I'll never judge you!' Mr Hosni gave a small sob and turned the boy to the mirror, smiling brokenly. 'Look at yourself, baby!' He shook the boy's shoulders until Dhurgham smiled wanly at the image of his lean little body covered in suds, his half erect penis and the lump of foam sliding from his hair. Mr Hosni towelled him dry, wrapped him up and carried him to the sitting room. He cuddled the boy until he fell asleep.

This boy, he thought, would feel loved and would never be deserted or cast out or shunned. This boy would be truly loved. 'To love, not to destroy and humiliate, Hani,' he said out loud to himself, happily.

It was as if a perfect boy had been born whole, aged twelve, and handed to Mr Hosni to be his very own.

The next time Dhurgham had a bath, Mr Hosni took a video. Dhurgham begged him not to but when Mr Hosni looked hurt he didn't have the energy to refuse. Mr Hosni brightened immediately and that evening transferred the images to his computer, chirping, 'Don't worry, Birdie, buck up! These are private for you and me—I'll never send these to anyone, I promise.'

Dhurgham saw the video once. He was ill with shame, made worse by Mr Hosni's great tenderness towards him. The footage was grainy and ugly. His thin body stood out white in the shadows, his face was averted and his eyes down. It didn't look manly.

The thought of it sapped his strength.

Mr Hosni's mother visited. Mrs Abboud was a large, stern woman who stayed only five minutes. She kissed Mr Hosni, gave him a large plastic bag full of dishes wrapped in alfoil and asked Dhurgham to show her out and walk her to the corner. She said nothing to him all the way, but when they parted, she grabbed him by the chin, twisted his face up to hers and searched it for something. Dhurgham met her glance because, for all that, she was not a scary lady. She gave him a strange, sad smile and tossed his face away, patting his back to go home.

When he got in, he noticed first a wonderful smell. He found Mr Hosni in the sitting room, wracked by sobs over an array of dishes, savouries and sweets, and an Eid card.

'They hate me,' Mr Hosni mouthed indistinctly through a raw and ugly wail. 'I haven't seen my father since I was twenty-five.' He rocked back and forth, and Dhurgham squatted at his side, not knowing what to do. 'I broke his heart. Oh, my Mother! Yamo Yamo Yamo!' Mr Hosni rocked and sobbed harder, and Dhurgham began to weep, half scared at seeing an adult like this.

'Mother Mother Mother,' he murmured too, his voice catching in his throat.

Mr Hosni's wails faded and stopped. They stayed sitting together in front of the TV. Mr Hosni placed his arm around Dhurgham's small body.

'You are a sweet, sweet, sweet boy. Well brought up too. I think I might adopt you.'

Dhurgham shut his eyes and leant into that warm armpit.

After that he and Mr Hosni slipped into an easier relationship. Mr Hosni usually slung his arm over Dhurgham's shoulders in front of the TV and both were comforted. Mr Hosni managed to get an Internet connection through one of his influential friends and was inordinately proud of being one of the first private Internet users in Damascus, although terrified of being monitored by the secret police. He paid for it and for protection from the authorities with Dhurgham's money. Dhurgham learnt how to use it under Mr Hosni's guidance. It was something that he had always dreamed of learning. They giggled together over naked women, and Mr Hosni stroked Dhurgham's blushing ears.

'You haven't seen much of Damascus, Birdie. I'll give you a proper education. I'll take you to all the great places.'

They only ever went to the gloomy Roman theatre at Busra but the promise hung in the air and Dhurgham leant in close in front of the TV at night.

With Mr Hosni, Dhurgham slowly healed. His bony thinness gave way to a fine leanness. He grew. His blank-eyed look appeared less often, his hair shone, he slept through the night and in time stopped taking tablets. He began to get the energy to be bored and to chafe at the intensely domestic life they led, although he remained too low-spirited to do anything about it. Their days together were filled with not much. Mr Hosni made him sit at the computer and play games while he did a modicum of work repairing electronics and managing his digital printing in the room upstairs. Mr Hosni cooked him breakfast and lunch, and usually took him out to dinner. Mr Hosni took him shopping or just strolling to the post office on Said al Jabri Avenue to collect or post his clients' orders, and to the bank to check their deposits and telegraphic transfers.

Mr Hosni loved his fruit to be perfect and his tomatoes firm. His spinach had to be perky. Their twice-weekly trips to the fresh produce souq could take up a whole day as Mr Hosni chattered and dithered over his choices, exclaiming in delight over the smell of mandarins today and the unblemished apples, or clicking his tongue in disappointment when he could find no peaches he approved of. Mr Hosni had his favourite place to shop for everything and disparaged any competitors of his chosen shops and stallholders as though shopping were a sport and he determined that his team should win. He taught Dhurgham how to choose everything with the right care and attention, what to look for, what to smell for, and how to tap a watermelon; but he nonetheless never let Dhurgham do the shopping by himself. Mr Hosni rarely let him even wander off by himself.

Dhurgham's bottom hurt. He sat at the table looking at Mr Hosni from under his lashes, but Mr Hosni seemed exactly the same as every morning—cheerful, warm and unreadable, preparing breakfast for them both.

Mr Hosni was in a good mood, better than usual, but careful to maintain his usual exterior. He hummed, as he often did, snatches of songs that made Dhurgham want to cry. Umm Kulthoum, his father's favourite, and Suad Massi, Nooni's.

Mr Hosni was secretly delighted. The boy was so young, so soft, so easy, so beautiful. He loved him, he really did. It was much better this way, better the boy know everything from his nearest and dearest, rather than get held down by strangers and forced. The boy was too beautiful to leave innocent in this terrible world, he needed to be able to protect himself and to choose the good from the bad. There were some dreadful people out there. Mr Hosni couldn't bear the thought. And the boy, he could tell, was ready. So beautiful and loving.

Dhurgham kept his eyes down, unnerved, and longing for Mr Hosni to hug him or murmur something in a deep voice in his ear, something to make the pain all right. Perhaps Mr Hosni would apologise. He would say it was a mistake, that he was a bad man but would never be bad again with his beloved boy.

Mr Hosni smiled and suddenly reached across the table, gripped Dhurgham's chin between thumb and forefinger and lifted the face until the black eyes met his.

'You are a grown-up, Birdie, in charge of your own money. Getting screwed is part of love, grown-up love. Much better with someone who loves you than with a bad man. Now be a man about it!'

Dhurgham sat up and twisted his face out of Mr Hosni's hand. He couldn't meet Mr Hosni's eyes and the words failed on his lips but he had a sudden revelation in all the mist that his father would kill Mr Hosni for this, and he felt himself strengthen as he tried to lean inward onto the memory of his father. Then a fiery wave of shame burned through his body and he thought—*I can never tell my father this*. He sat stiffly, waiting for Mr Hosni to saunter out, waiting for space to think unscrutinised. But Mr Hosni hovered, invading, bucking him up, being nice to him, staring at him; and soon, in a strange way, Dhurgham wanted him to stay, to somehow take away the burden that overwhelmed him. So they spent the whole day together and, by nightfall, Dhurgham had talked too much and had suffered enough kindnesses from Mr Hosni to know that he no longer had the upper hand, no longer could kill him, really, as Mr Hosni had been too good to him. Mr Hosni told him that he was a well brought-up boy, and this praise of himself and most of all his parents softened him still more. They went to their separate beds and both slept dreamlessly.

Dhurgham smashed up the entire neat kitchen on the second day, breaking everything that was breakable, including the table and chairs and the lights, then paid for it out of his money to a thin-lipped Mr Hosni by candlelight. He then slipped into a hazy, self-hating acceptance.

Mr Hosni changed tactic. He told Dhurgham that his family were dead, held him tight and patted his head, and then adopted a more fatherly tone and role with him, never reminding him of his adulthood and never reminding him of love. Dhurgham craved this remission into childhood so profoundly that he was prepared to pay for it with adult love in the dark once a fortnight or so. He quickly learned not to think about it, to see it as a kind of uncomfortable dream, and he appreciated how Mr Hosni respected this. He appreciated, too, how Mr Hosni cuddled him long afterwards as though he was a little boy who had had a confusing nightmare.

• • •

A year passed. Dhurgham was a more silent boy than he had been—he had more to think about. His body lengthened and strengthened. He and Mr Hosni never spoke about money and never spoke about the fairly rare evenings that saw Mr Hosni slide his soft and perfumed body into the single bed and curl in close behind Dhurgham. Dhurgham fantasised about running away and about joining an army. He wondered how much money was left and whether he could just ask to see it, then take it and walk out the door. But he owed Mr Hosni too much; and he wanted Mr Hosni to like him, to think well of him and to love him.

Mr Hosni no longer looked at himself in wonderment. For him it was a happy time. Perhaps the happiest time of his life. He provided Dhurgham with everything and could see that the boy was grateful—no pushy urchin, this one.

He had seen his birdie glow in almost angry embarrassed pleasure when he praised that beautiful painting. He lay awake thinking about how changed his life was, now that he had someone to care for, someone to love. And Dhurgham was special, talented. Gifted, even. Maybe a Van Gogh. Mr Hosni felt ennobled; he could truly say he loved someone who was not his mother or father. The boy would understand, in time, especially when he saw more of the world. He would be careful to make sure his boy only went with the decent, gentle types. He'd be just like a father whose daughter had started dating. He would watch over his boy, yes he would.

It was in a way a settled time. Dhurgham said little as Mr Hosni took him to parties and gatherings. Dhurgham dressed to please Mr Hosni, and Mr Hosni swelled with pride to have his well-groomed, tall, exquisite nephew at his side.

'I was such a sad man,' he said happily to Dhurgham late one night as they walked home through the unlit alleys. 'I can see that now. But with you in my life, I feel much better.'

Mr Hosni broke the spell. They were sitting on the living-room floor watching television. President Bush's son was trying to get elected but no one wanted him. The hilariously named Al Gore was going to win. Mr Hosni switched off the television, breaking their routine, and Dhurgham's heart fluttered painfully in his chest.

'Birdie, your money has run out. There is none left. How are you going to pay for your board and food?'

'That's impossible!' Dhurgham looked trapped. It couldn't be. There had been so much of it!

'You are expensive! It's more than *possible*, it *is*!'

Dhurgham couldn't speak.

'You will have to work, but what can a pretty, soft youth with no trade do?' Mr Hosni said gently.

Dhurgham wanted to cry out. His family had nothing. Their money could no longer keep him. How had this happened?

I have a trade, I have a trade. I can read and write. I am good at art. I know the Internet!

But he couldn't make a sound.

'I have some friends who will help us, don't worry,' Mr Hosni said soothingly. 'We won't have to do much, and I'll make sure they are only the good ones. It's what most people do, you know, but not many have their old Uncle looking after everything.'

Dhurgham stared at him wild-eyed, suddenly seeing just how trapped he was. He looked around. He ran into the kitchen and scooped up all the bread and the water jug and a jar of jam, with Mr Hosni trailing him in bewilderment. Then, sobbing with his inability to run, Dhurgham clambered upstairs, feeling weak, as if caught into the fabric of one of his own dreams. He barricaded his door from the inside. He sat, shaking and dizzy, on the bed, aware of how afraid of Mr Hosni's disappointment, hurt or anger he was; and how little he knew what his benefactor's reaction would be. Mr Hosni climbed the stairs and Dhurgham's heart thumped against the top of his stomach. Sweat leapt out all over his body. Mr Hosni tried the door, softly, then nothing. Dhurgham knew he was just outside, thinking. He buried his head between his knees to stop himself from fainting. Then he heard his benefactor sigh and tread heavily down the stairs, and he breathed more easily.

He felt foolish. Here he was barricaded in an upstairs room of his only friend's house, with enough food to last perhaps three days. He felt very foolish and small. But he didn't open the door, and he swore to himself that there would be no more adult love, no more, because, even though he felt the reasonableness of Mr Hosni's argument, he also felt its unfairness, its meanness, and he was on fire, finally, with an anger that could find no words.

He curled up on the bed, thinking, *I have a trade, I have! I am a great pilot, and philosophers also come in handy, as do artists*. He escaped for a while imagining a scenario in which Mr Hosni discovered that he was a real pilot. Mr Hosni was terribly impressed and got Dhurgham to smuggle things, trusting him on his honour to return.

He stayed the three days in his room, thinking; pissing, first out of the window, then into the empty water jug. When he descended to the kitchen on the fourth day, he was sweating again but exhilarated in his fear.

Mr Hosni was seated at the table. He lifted his head and whispered, 'Birdie!' He had tears on his cheeks, but Dhurgham had only one plan and only one chance. He looked away so as not to be twisted. He walked over to the table and leant forward without sitting down, aware for the very first time of his own height.

'My name is Dhurgham,' he said. 'Never call me Birdie again.'

Mr Hosni smiled and Dhurgham was thrown by his benefactor's assurance. He leant in closer, trying to cover his fear.

Mr Hosni raised both hands, palms upward in capitulation. 'Okay Birdie, okay. It's Dhurgham from now on. You are the man.'

'And no more photos. Ever.'

'OK, no problem—I didn't know you minded.'

'I will pay my rent and board when I can. Until then you can love, once a fortnight. But not in my bed. And I choose … when.'

Mr Hosni shook his head slowly and smiled sadly.

'Birdie, you don't know the going rates for love. That is nowhere near enough!'

Dhurgham began to shake so hard that Mr Hosni could see it. Mr Hosni's smile broadened. He stood up.

'Have it your way,' he said lightly. 'I don't mind. I love you dearly. You are like a son to me.'

Dhurgham crumpled into his seat and Mr Hosni made him pancakes for breakfast.

From then on, on rare occasions when Mr Hosni asked Dhurgham to stay a day or two with one of his friends, Dhurgham did so without a word. His great debt mounted and his self-disgust kept him passive. Mr Hosni never even had to mention it.

Meanwhile Dhurgham's body grew. He was already tall at thirteen. At Eid in his fourteenth year, Mr Hosni gave him a set of dumbbells.

Dhurgham remembered his bedroom, suddenly, as potently as if he could curl into his quilt, open his eyes and there it would be. His mind reached inward, yearning for the distant clank and tinkle of his street, the heavy scrape of his door, the smell of wood and kerosene in the entrance, then up the stairs, round the corner, up again to the landing, to his room. He could see the golden light on the walls, could smell the familiar mix of old socks, plastic toys, oiled wood and orange blossom wafting in from the orchard. That season, again. He wanted to cry. Every detail, so ordinary then, so unremarked, was radiant and painful in his mind, emblematic. His budgie chirruped from the cage on the sill. Yes! His yellow Susie! His refugee from the bombings. The war had given him Susie when he was just five. Clinging yellow to his windowsill, and so afraid. Her wings were translucent white. How could he have forgotten Susie?

He could see his toys, scattered about, each one speaking of his loss. He could hear the hum and clatter of the house, the loud clink outside of the gas vendor. He could hear, almost touch, almost smell, what he once was. His happiness.

Mr Hosni dragged Dhurgham with him by the hand. Dhurgham could feel Mr Hosni sweating, could feel Mr Hosni's fear.

'Come with, come with. I can't see him without your help! I can't!' Mr Hosni gasped. Spittle bubbled at the centre of his bottom lip and sobs rose from his chest. Dhurgham shuddered with feelings he couldn't define. He wanted to pull away, stand up, but he didn't pull his hand away from the frenetic tugging and clutching of Mr Hosni's hands, pulling him down into a stoop. Mr Hosni was doubled over in terror.

They got to the hospital door and then Mr Hosni passed out as he stepped over the threshold. He just stumbled as though he had tripped, then slid down and flopped to the ground at Dhurgham's feet. Dhurgham stood next to him, helplessly, as medical staff rushed over. The puff of cold hospital air had paralysed him with memories. He hoped they would find something seriously wrong with Mr Hosni and keep him. He thought vaguely that he could simply walk away now.

'He's just upset,' Dhurgham said distantly. 'His father is dying.'

• • •

He stayed with Mr Hosni as if in a dream. He stood quietly by as Mr Hosni sobbed into Mrs Abboud's chest. He was with them, silent, when they went to the huge stone house on the outskirts of Damascus which Mr Hosni had not seen since he was twenty-five. He sat wordless in the back of the car as Mr Hosni's mother drove them home the day after the burial. He said nothing, shocked, when Mrs Abboud took his hand in hers, placed her other hand over it and, holding tightly, said, 'Look after my Hani, his heart will break now.' And then he held Mr Hosni as he seemed to spread wide and soggy on the floor. Now and then Mr Hosni lay down, curled on the floor, shaking all over, but mostly he just sobbed and filled the room with used tissues. The long threads of hair that normally trailed over his balding scalp hung down on one side to his shoulder. Dhurgham said nothing. He had one clear memory to focus on. He was feeling for its edges, feeling for a tiny crack he could peel back to uncover his family.

He had only been to a hospital once. He was ten. Uncle Mahmoud was yellow and his bones stood out under the skin. The cut in his belly was blue and puffy like a stitched quilt. It was the fattest thing on him. He could see Uncle Mahmoud pointing to his belly, lifting his shirt with a bony yellow elbow held high. He could hear Uncle Mahmoud's voice. 'I got here and said, where is the sheet on my bed? They said, you have to bring your own. Then I said, where is my blanket? You have to bring your own. Then dinner came round, lentil soup. Goodie, I thought. Then they said, where is your bowl, you should have brought one with you. So I couldn't have soup, and next day, when Umm Jamal brought me a bowl, there was no more soup. Then they did the operation because I was starved enough and a doctor happened by on his way to the West. When I woke up, three days later, because they use horse anaesthetic, I said, where is my nurse? What do you mean, nurse? they said, you have to bring your own.'

Uncle Mahmoud joked as usual, but his mouth, stretched thin and dry over his teeth, made it seem as though he wasn't really joking. He smelt bad. It was the last time Dhurgham saw Uncle Mahmoud. He knew that without remembering anything more.

There was no chink, no lifting corner. Nothing that took him out of the hospital, away from Uncle Mahmoud's dying. It was seamless. Even Nooni, who must have been standing beside him next to the iron bed, was erased. Why was it that his memories were stripped from him? Mr Hosni, sleeping now with jagged childlike breaths, was indecent with the grief of his memories. Dhurgham looked down at his benefactor. He felt the weight of that head in his lap and he imagined it dead, brains rotting under the thin hair.

'That boy will turn on you, you know,' Mr Hilton said softly to Mr Hosni as he watched Dhurgham serve them. 'He'll add it all up one day soon and probably stab you in your bed.' There was a certain smugness to his voice that made Mr Hosni dismiss what he had said.

'You are jealous. The boy loves me. He is my nephew.'

'He's not your nephew. You've told me as much yourself. Who calls a child "Dhurgham" these days anyway? He's an upper-class Baghdadi, who arrived at your doorstep laden with money. No doubt in Syria illegally. What does that make him, Hani?'

'You tell me.'

'A liability. Get rid of him before he grows to manhood and takes a close look at you.'

Mr Hosni laughed. But later he worried over Mr Hilton's words. Mr Hilton was no Damascene. He was one of those strange British men who had travelled all over, including, in Mr Hilton's case, Baghdad, and who then stayed semipermanently, settling in to a world in which their outsider status and diplomatic connections were just enough for them to live outside the law; and their knowledge, experience, contacts and practised Arabic were enough to give them access to subterranean circles. He was a procurer, a man who gave other westerners tours. Mr Hosni had kept Dhurgham well away from that circle, protecting him from such men, and Mr Hilton was, he was sure, offended. But

Mr Hilton knew more than he was letting on. Maybe he even recognised the boy. Maybe Mr Hilton would try to poison his birdie's mind against him. And Mr Hosni was startled to realise that he had never really thought about what would happen when Dhurgham grew up and thought about everything. Would Dhurgham really see it his way? Could the boy hate him for what he had done? There was the money—but what was money when it came to love? He could not desert the boy. He had never felt such love for anyone. Did his boy love him in return?

He thought hard about it. The reaction to his announcement that the money was gone had always irked him. If the boy loved him, would he have cared so much? Birdie had really failed that test. Mr Hosni had always comforted himself that the other suggestion had triggered it and had been cross with himself for bringing that up at the same time. But what if some vestige of the boy's past still tainted him?

Mr Hosni worried for three nights. The problem of Dhurgham grew in urgency the more attention he gave it. What would happen? Could Dhurgham creep into this room in the darkness with a shining knife in his hand? Mr Hosni felt a frisson of delicious, sensual fear. Then he felt spooked. After the romantic image, there would of course be the plunging knife, again and again, the convulsion and then … oblivion. His mother's tears. He lay quiet, thinking more coldly. If not the knife, then what? The Police? This thought filled him with a cold, leaden fear. There was nothing sensual about al Mazzeh prison.

He had to get rid of him. But the boy would be better off dead than cast out. Unwanted and betrayed. No. That would be too cruel. And he had sworn he would never cast him out. In the early hours of the third morning he almost screwed up his courage to organise the boy's disappearance. But it was a phantom. As soon as he put the proposition seriously to himself, he knew that he couldn't possibly really contemplate it. Then, at the call to prayer of the third dawn, he had an inspiration.

Mr Hosni knew he would miss Dhurgham, but with the threat of Dhurgham's manhood disrupting everything, even proving dangerous, he couldn't keep him.

He slept all morning. It was perfect.

At breakfast, a week later, Mr Hosni let himself look appropriately tired, drawn and worried. Dhurgham noticed straight away.

'Sit down, Birdie.'

Dhurgham sat opposite Mr Hosni at the kitchen table, as they had so many times before.

Mr Hosni leant forward. Tears started involuntarily in his eyes. He really did feel immeasurably sad. He blenched and said in a low voice, 'They have found you out. They know who you are. We have to get you out of the country as soon as possible!' He watched with inner satisfaction as Dhurgham jumped fearfully.

Dhurgham stared speechless, his eyes wide. The past seemed so dreamy, such an unlikely story to carry with one as a half-held memory. And 'they' had always been shadowy, dream figures. But what opened in his heart was a trickle, then a growing clamour for action, for leaving. It was as if Mr Hosni had painted a door on a picture, and said, *Go on, open it*. His heart thumped, and he watched his benefactor suspiciously.

'I know a man, a *Mr Leon*,' Mr Hosni said, leaning forward and whispering the name, then sitting back again. 'I've paid for *everything*, because I love you, B— Dhurgham. I am sending you to a new life in Australia. You leave in two days. Once you are settled, you might send for me, your old Uncle, send me a visa—' He trailed off in a daydream. Birdie would never blame him. Birdie would have a new life, in a country where a boy could have a real job and would forget bad things. Birdie might marry and name his firstborn Hani … The plan was absolutely perfect. He felt so good about himself that the expense didn't bother him. He noted this with surprise and pleasure. Yes, that was it! No expense would be spared. A strangely enchanting sadness filled him. He had never felt quite so virtuous, quite so much the hero character—relinquishing all, selflessly, and righting wrongs at the same time. Dhurgham would love him, always. Alone in the kitchen, after Dhurgham went

53

out for a walk, he sat silent, more sad now than happy. It was going to be a lonely house.

Dhurgham went first to the mosque. He hadn't been there for nearly two years. It looked smaller and grimier than he remembered, until he entered. The vista of the great courtyard opened up, vast and calm, the marble flagstones gleaming. He walked around the arcades slowly, glancing cursorily at all the familiar textures and images. He felt nothing at all. He could remember all this and it seemed that it had nothing to say to him now, or that it was unwilling to give him anything for his journey. He left again in minutes, vaguely relieved and disappointed.

He walked with long strides without direction through the streets. Slowly, he began to feel dizzy with joy, as if his legs were making huge bounds that were the clumsy preliminaries to graceful take-off, to long-distance migratory flight to the south. To the West. To the lands of the setting sun. *Australia*.

He was going to see a kangaroo.

He found himself on a street that seemed familiar —not from his time with Mr Hosni; this was a street of dreams, not of the real world. This was a street from before the mosque, his earliest clear point of continuous memory. His heart hammered and he felt sick and dizzy. Then he felt a stranger's sad kiss burn into his forehead before he even fully remembered. He crept stealthily along the street, sneaking up on his memories, on lost secrets. He came to a stop in front of the safe house before he recognised it.

He stared up at a blackened, pock-marked façade. It was a shell, burnt out and uninhabited. Destroyed some time before and overgrown with weeds. Part of the high wall was pushed down, as if by a bulldozer. The front door was gone, the interior fire-scarred in the shadows. He had a sudden revelation that his fleeting seconds on this same pavement two and a half years before had marked the house. That this was all part of his story and he had only the flimsiest hold on who he was in the world. The loss washed over him, pummelled him before he could deflect it. He was choking, again, again. A passing old man with broken teeth chanted in a singsong voice, '*Tears of parting sorrow over the cold ash of the beloved's campfire,*' and then winked at him. 'You're too young, sonny!'

He walked away, still feeling the ghostly press of Ali's lips, feeling his sight darken and blister, and his legs weaken.

Who was Ali? *Who was Dhurgham Mohammad As-Samarra'i?*

II

hurgham stepped off the plane into a buffet of humid heat. Indonesia. Indonesia leapt in to greet him with the call of the muezzin floating over lush green palms, heady green verges. Green. He felt the joy of it course through him. He was just fourteen; he was in a new land, beginning a new life. He had been on an aeroplane for the first time in his life. He could feel Damascus leaving him like an old stink peeling off under a hot shower.

He walked into the sudden cool of the terminal building with the others and stood with a kind of happy uncertainty in a sequence of queues.

The Indonesian official looked him in the eye and stamped his false passport without looking at it. Dhurgham came down to earth. He walked away with something nagging him. That official, he *knew*. His happy sense of freedom drained away. Mr Hosni and Mr Leon had of course arranged it.

Finding Mr Leon's contact in the car park was easy. A cluster of bewildered Iraqi and Afghan boys, covered women and shy, exhausted-looking children huddled together, eyeing everyone who passed. A dirty white minibus pulled up with Hotel Intan Sunray written on the side in English. The lettering formed the calyx of a magenta and orange flower. They were herded on by a hand-flapping Indonesian who seemed to know only rude words in Arabic. Their driver, by contrast, spoke Arabic and Dari, and said everything in both. Mr Leon, their driver said, had it all arranged. Mr Leon was the best travel agent, the best. They would be staying at the beautiful Hotel Intan Sunray in glorious Indonesia. They were to relax, recuperate until their boat was made ready to take them to freedom and prosperity in Australia.

'Boat?' a voice interjected with a rising inflection. She was a thin young woman in chador, clutching two children in a white-knuckled grip.

'Not boat, madame—ship! A Titanic, with three swimming pools,' the driver said waggishly, 'Not to forget the bathers!'

The Hotel Intan Sunray was halfway between a hotel and a hostel. It was owned, their driver had said, by Mr Leon's brother-in-law. It was beautiful to Dhurgham but he couldn't enjoy it. All the staff knew. He heard 'taliby-l-luju', 'asylum seekers', muttered here and there.

He became acutely conscious of the difference between his clothing and that of genuine tourists. He blushed as only fourteen year olds can over his sneakers, his jeans, his shirt, his hairstyle, his downy upper lip, his Arab eyes, his language, his overgrown fingernails and his lack of swimming trunks. He pestered his fellow travellers for a set of nailclippers and made a mess of his own hair trying to cut it. He tried to wear a keffiyeh to cover his damaged hair but took it off almost in tears after he got a filthy look from a beautiful American backpacker. The week spent on the gracious lawns and around the shining pool, in the foyer under the woodcarvings or with six others in the room, was agony.

The food was strange—rice, bean shoots, peanut sauce. He was curious and asked what everything was. He ate everything. He stole the menu in the restaurant of the Hotel Intan Sunray and pored over it, wondering at the impenetrable array of strangeness that might be laid out for him to try. *Nasi Campur, Selada Ayam, Lumpia, Gado-Gado.* The menu was bound by a green ribbon. The front cover showed a green terraced mountain with huge blooms and bamboo in the foreground, with people working near palm trees, backs bent, in the middle distance. Nothing could make Indonesia seem real to him. Even these fellaheen, working hard in the fields, were considered picturesque, ornamental.

The words on street signs were a strange language in European letters. He had enough English from primary school to see which bits were English but not enough to know exactly what they said or meant. *Safari Taylor*, one sign said; another, *Big Enjoy: Ketut Raja, Wood Carver*. Indonesian was somehow soft and ringing at the same time. Words of greeting were almost Arabic, familiar and strange, their known shapes wrapped in strange mouths and altered.

The throng on the beach was very quiet. The sun shone on the glittering blue water. Out towards the horizon Dhurgham could see that the ocean was speckled with white. Coloured pennants lined the sandy track behind them and snapped faintly in the breeze, swaying on their bamboo poles. Chickens pecked without ardour under the palm copses at the edge of the sand, ignoring the crowd. He had expected that their boat would be special, bigger and more modern than the fishing boats he had seen. He had a mental picture of something with sleek lines, white-hulled and with blue striping. Something clearly made for speed, as indestructible as a bullet and of course large enough to have a swimming pool. And beyond all this, he had expected it to be marked as special for him. It would have a special name and would be rigged with arcane Indonesian charms and silk flags fluttering in the breeze. It would have music and some strange, foreign ceremony which recognised that it was to carry a cargo beyond price to a new land. It would be charged with the nobility of its mission and the glory of the dangers it would face and overcome. Whatever their individual stories, he knew by now that his fellow travellers shared something. The boat would make the crossing from despair to hope; for some, from death to life.

He did not believe the fishing boat was their boat even as they were harried into the warm water to wade out to it. It was exactly the same as all the other larger fishing boats he had seen tossing and tugging at their ropes in the bay. It had the same battered, flaking blue paint, the same weathered wood, low gunwale and open deck. It was larger than it looked—once he had clambered and slithered aboard in his wet clothes, he found that it also had a lower hold rigged with a decking floor, in which most people could just stand. He had to stoop a little to fit. Even as they headed out towards that gaily speckled ocean, Dhurgham and some others kept looking for the boat they thought they were being ferried to.

The *Hibiscus* stank of fish and fuel of some kind. Its upper deck was spattered with grey stains—fish blood and grease. The lower deck was clearly new. It was filthy but the timber was a light, faint gold.

Dhurgham assumed that there would be men who would take charge, who would see to the supplies and the boat in general. Men had loaded them all on. By the time land was almost out of sight and lunchtime hunger had set in, he realised that there were no men on board the *Hibiscus*. The boat was full of older boys from Afghanistan, boys from Iraq, small boys, scared boys. What was it, that their boat had only boys? There were maybe fifteen children younger than Dhurgham; the rest, all boys, mostly older. Hundreds of boys. His unease increased. He scanned the beardless faces and the tiny moustaches, stared into the eager, unsure eyes, some Arab, some Asiatic, but all the same. Even the helmsman couldn't have been more than eighteen and had an uncertain look and a habit of waving 360 degrees when asked their direction.

The three Indonesians wore futas, making them look older, old-fashioned, or maybe just different from the boys, but Dhurgham eyed them sur-reptitiously—they looked no more than eighteen or nineteen as well. Older than him but not confident. It was surreal, frightening. What had happened to the world while he was in Syria? Who would send sons away like this? What had happened that it was safer to set precious boys adrift rather than keep them home?

Supplies were, given their numbers, minimal. They had fifteen plastic tubs of water, a cooking oven, some unpleasant-smelling oil, two bags of oranges, several filthy pans and a large sack of rice. No one seemed to be in charge. One of the Indonesian boys lit the burner and began cooking rice. Then they took turns cooking in shifts, without thinking, as rice had to be cooking almost all the time to feed them.

On the third day, with no land in sight, they stopped cooking. There was no more rice. The oranges were long gone. The water was more than half gone and the boys each separately thought about rationing, but none felt himself to be able to put it into action.

One of the bigger boys began rationing water too late, guarding it fiercely with a big stick. They all dropped back into their boyhoods, nursing their hunger and thirst but relieved.

The helmsman put a young Afghan boy at the wheel and went to sleep curled up on the deck.

The journey, gentle and all erasing, seemed too dreamy to be real. Dhurgham could feel the strength of the ocean each time it lifted the boat, then its boredom as it dropped it. He stared down into the sliding sea and could see only a starburst of waterlight, following, maybe even made by, his eye. It was constant; there with its vanishing centre whenever he looked. He couldn't see the bottom. Looking into the sea made him feel blind. He couldn't see a thing that had a meaning. He could hear someone weeping through the wooden slats of the cabin near his right shoulder, and he could hear sandals slapping and sneakers shuffling on the grey wooden deck as older boys and small boys passed back and forth, stepping over him as they made their way to the bow.

A cry rose up from the front and, looking down, he saw it too, speeding across the fluttering lines of light and giving the water dimension again. A dolphin. A giant fish. As it broke the water he wondered idly what it would be like to live in water. To breathe it. To break the surface and crash through it again, home. Then he wondered what dolphin tasted like just as a hundred other boys had the same thought and began to throw things at it in desperate excitement. Then it was gone.

Juicy white flesh, huge amounts of it, breaking away from the bone in handfuls, slabs, sweet and flaky. A burning fire and solid ground, and a feast of fish, scented lightly with coriander, lemon and chilli, garlic-glazed, gripped in the hand with strips of soft, layered fenugreek-sprinkled flatbread. Fish!

He huddled around his stomach longing for rice and stared again into the water. Those radiant lines were not reaching out from a point but leading to it in the far far deeps.

The weather held. The sea stayed blue and mountainous, the sky whisked with high cloud. The sea was infinitely variable and infinitely boring. Dhurgham sat long hours in a kind of slow-motion shock. Could this be what Mr Hosni intended and what Mr Leon planned? Could this be the orderly world of adults, finally revealed to be something else: uncertain, frightening, life-sapping, life-threatening? Could they really be as vulnerable as they seemed? What would his father think about this final journey that his son was making? If his mother, if Nura could see him now, they would scream in terror—why? Why? He could not find his centre, find his peace, find any rock on which to ground himself and calm the electric jolt that coursed through him. He gripped white-knuckled to the flaking gunwale.

His unease slowly quieted as he watched the water. He let go and put his hands flat to the scored whorls of the warm grey timber on which he sat. He shivered in the heat and felt his mind and heart go numb. He huddled in a self-protective bubble; not thinking, not feeling.

Most of the boys were ill and so weak they could not make it to the side to dry retch. The smell and the heat below deck were intolerable. Some of the older boys fought over leadership. Some played games of strength and skill. Most made small, weak bundles and fell silent. It was all too dreamy for Dhurgham to do more than look on. He became vaguely aware that the engine was no longer going just as there was an uproar over it. Nothing touched him. He watched three bigger boys drop a dead Afghan boy over the side but was as blank as the sea, feeling nothing more than the flickering of light in his eyes.

He had a lot of time. Slowly, as his panic settled, he began to think. His mind worked slowly and increasingly methodically through his memories. There could be no doubt that there was something wrong with him. There were such impenetrable fog banks not so far back. He could follow himself as a small, luminous figure, a feeling, seeing centre, rich in days and nights and countless memories, right up to the brink of fog, and then … nothing. Fear and horror. A van. Marsh birds. He could barely remember the safe house as it had been before it was destroyed, but he could almost see it, at the very edge of that fog. And way back before the fog, he still had something of his childhood with him. Nura. Ahmad. His father. Mother. Colours and vague experiences. A whole world that he would retrieve if he could but travel back through that fog and dispel it. It seemed so simple.

He stared at the waves. Each was different. Each was identical. He watched the light play through and over them. It was as though an altogether different light played from within the waves, and sunlight itself was the lesser, more fickle light. The deep blue far under each wave had something to say. The waves lifted and curled and folded, over and over; each simple and each so detailed, intricate in its lines and shadows, in its form and sliding myriad colours, that it would take him his lifetime to paint them. This blue slide here, amazingly fringed in liquid pink, repeated here, here, here! This green line, again and again. This silver; this gold.

The waves, for all their motion, resembled the mosaic.

He flooded with grief and grace at the same moment. He alone, in all the world, was the living point at which such a truth could be made manifest, for he was the only creature ever to absorb both into his being.

The sea now stilled to a silken shimmer. The boat slid along the ocean on an unseen current. To Dhurgham it seemed as if it were hovering, rocking on slow wing beats, carrying him as if by accident and yet by such design! The lift of the boat, the buoyancy that held him in the air, seemed charged with its glory and purpose. How funny that he had wanted it to have pennants and insignias when of course it had to be this plain, this battered, this invisible to others!

The boys had slowly retreated from one another and entered their own private dreams. Some had rigged up small shade cloths; others just slipped to the deck, backs to the gunwale, and stayed there.

Dhurgham's father's voice flowed suddenly from the boy slumped next to him, ringing and clear.

'In the Name of God, the Compassionate, the Merciful: when the sun ceases to shine; when the stars fall down and the mountains are blown away—'

Dhurgham began to weep. His huge happiness bubbled up and he joined his cracked whisper to that beautiful voice.

'—when camels big with young are left untended, and the wild beast are brought together; when the seas are set alight and men's souls are reunited; when the infant girl buried alive is asked for what crime she was slain; when the records of men's deeds are laid open, and heaven is stripped bare—'

The whispers crackled and sighed and warmed up until the whole upper deck was quietly murmuring.

'—when Hell burns fiercely and Paradise is brought near: then each soul shall know what it has done.'

His father's voice faded and vanished into the blue. Nura stepped lightly over the supine boys towards him.

'Don't mind Dad. He sees Judgement Day in everything. We are going to the West and he thinks it's the end of the world!'

Dhurgham laughed. Dad did, he really did. It was so funny!

Nura dropped down next to him.

'When the embargo ends, let's travel the world—'

'And the Two Seas—'

'We'll go to America—'

'And see bears—'

'And Russia, France and Australia. Let's go to uni in a different country every year, and wear different clothes in each place. Chic clothes.'

'We'll go on roller-coasters.'

'We'll have two freezers that can't break down.'

'We'll have a garden that never withers because it will have a spring, and it'll be full of birds of every colour!'

'Watered by running streams; eternal are its fruits and eternal are its shades—'

The boys around him listened closely, murmuring sibilantly with the slap of the water against wood. Now their murmur swelled:

'—there shall be two other gardens of darkest green. Which of your Lord's blessings would you deny?

'A gushing fountain shall flow in each. Which of your Lord's blessings would you deny?

'Each planted with fruit trees, the palm and the pomegranate. Which of your Lord's blessings would you deny?'

A boy staggered onto the deck and said in Arabic, then in Dari, 'We are sinking.' A few boys clambered to their feet. Dhurgham felt a faint breath of annoyance at them for moving, then nothing again. He sought out the verse again and rode it onward to its conclusion.

He felt utterly still.

The great grey Australian ship neared. Dhurgham felt for a moment that his peace was broken. Then he felt relief and, slowly, slowly, in drips and drops, elation. The boys around him broke cracked lips open and waved, it seemed to him, far too fast. The ship's inflatable dingy bumped against the *Hibiscus*, jolting its rhythm, breaking its endless hovering, its eternal motion.

He stood, slowly, his back bent, supporting himself with one hand against the gunwale. 'Itnashr yawm!' someone croaked, weeping. Yes, if he thought about it, he knew they had been at sea twelve days. But he had

71

lived a whole life in his head and there really was not much need for more.

The beautiful navy officers, their faces shocked, tried to hug him and to carry him, but once he had stood up his body hurt too much to be touched.

The bus slowed into a small village just after dawn and turned off the highway. A fortified camp was visible in the distance almost straight away, but before it there was a very high metallic barrier across the road. This was soon clear as a set of gleaming double gates standing in the middle of nowhere, topped with coils of prison-like wire. No fence stretched to either side. These fortified open wings, standing there alone, marked an invisible border, a gateway to nothingness. *A-I-D* the sign said. And underneath: *Australian Immigration Department*. Then, in big block letters: WELCOME TO MAWIRRIGUN ALIENS PROCESSING CENTRE. Along the bottom of the sign was a cryptic imperative in a nicer, slanting font: *Advance Australia Fair*. Dhurgham saw that rolls of jagged wire lay at periodic intervals on the ground to either side, marking out a new perimeter fence line. Steel pylons lay in heaps, gleaming against the red earth, waiting to be erected. It was a half-built place and had something clandestine, makeshift, about the mix of unbuilt gleaming wire and the high inner fence. Work crews moved languidly in the middle distance. A golden-haired workman, bare torso copper in the early sun, stood by the sentinel gates and stared up at Dhurgham as the bus passed him. His deep-set blue eyes were inquiring, uncertain. His stare was so intense that Dhurgham felt something was demanded of him personally. He raised his hand. The beautiful young man involuntarily lifted his own, then dropped it to his side and frowned. They passed through a second perimeter fence, this one thoroughly solid, topped with barbed wire, and entered the dusty compound.

It was a prison, no doubt about that. Dhurgham was faintly surprised. He wondered fleetingly whether anyone knew him, then dismissed the possibility. No one here knew him or Mr Hosni. They were in *Australia*.

The double perimeter fence, the blade-threaded wire rolled at the top, the disdain on the guards' faces—none of these seemed real. He stood up tall and expanded his fourteen year old chest. He was in a new country, among new people, freed from the terrible boat journey, freed from the grim drone and shudder of the road trip and the huddle with the others in the alien buses. He was tens of thousands of miles away from Mr Hosni. The wire, and the desert surrounding it, were a simple impediment, a short insignificant hiatus to be handled with grace and fortitude. His eyes shone and the guards looked at him as though he were mad. The mothers looked and saw a beautiful baby in the long, too-thin body, but their hands and hearts were too full and their own fears too pressing to do more than note it.

Sometime on that first day in Mawirrigun Aliens Processing Centre, Dhurgham suddenly thought his parents might be here, right here—and, if not, then somewhere in this country. It was the first time in a long while that he had thought of them in the present and he was for a moment washed with guilt and a strange reluctance to bring them to life again, to feed his hope. He felt dizzy. Then to his horror he could not recall their faces. His mother's form, movement, voice; but not her face. Nura's hair. His father's cloak. No more. But he might see them, any minute now! He was only four weeks away from Damascus—they could so easily be here before him! His heart lurched with guilt, hope and pain; he peered through chinks and wire to get glimpses of the people who occupied the main part of the centre. He and the two hundred and seventy-three boys from the *Hibiscus* were held separately. Later he found out that this was to make sure no one helped them. If they failed to say the right words, they were slipped into the deportation quota without a hearing, staying in this isolation wing until, bewildered and afraid, they were flown out of the country again to who knows where. This weeded out many of the uneducated, several of the younger

74

children and all those who had not been as carefully briefed as Dhurgham. They were the unwanted the world over, he was later told.

The isolation wing was tense, with mothers rocking crying children, white-faced themselves at the indignities and petty cruelties some of the staff inflicted; bewildered by the kindness shown by others. One man sobbed, forbidden from contacting either his brother in Sydney or his family in Iraq in case someone helped him with the magic words. When he said that his family would not know whether he was dead or alive, an AID guard laughed. But this first day, Dhurgham was too happy and still too detached from the world to mind much. He merely noticed these things and remembered them later.

One by one, over several weeks, the boys of the *Hibiscus* were interviewed and were either left there to be deported or were sent into the main centre. The families from other boats could give no more information than the boys themselves had. No one in isolation knew why some were rejected and some accepted, as those who were accepted for processing didn't return to the isolation wing. One family ahead of Dhurgham were interviewed separately. The mother and the two daughters went straight into the main centre. The bewildered father and ten year old son returned and queued miserably every day for the interview they didn't understand was over.

Dhurgham was four weeks in isolation before he had his interview. He had stopped hoping that Nura was just the other side of the fence and had tried to calm himself to a rational expectancy. He had stopped straining to see whether he could catch a glimpse of his parents. He had once seen in the distance a slim woman in a white hijab with a very tall, willowy daughter and had told himself in rising excitement that Nooni would be grown up by now. His mother, he thought, might wear a white hijab now, thinking that he, Dhurgham, was dead. How exciting for them to discover him alive, to find what a journey he had made all by himself! But time dragged on and he tried to amuse himself by playing with the frustrated children who milled about, all well past their first fears and thoroughly bored. He was the only person unencumbered by stress and hardly tormented by the thought of a family elsewhere that might be yearning for news of him. It had been too long; and, if they were here, how he would surprise them! He was young and free. He could float around smiling, playful, untouched and giving.

In that first month, as the tension and bewilderment of their circumstances and the inexplicable behaviour of the guards had them all on edge and snappy, Dhurgham's bright, hopeful face and endless play with the children brought him close to many families. And in that first month he stayed somehow half detached and happy, rocked in the cradle of the terrible boat journey, remembering it with clarity, without fear, even occasionally with a strange pleasure.

His first interview was very brief. There was an interpreter, a middle-aged Lebanese man who looked at him in an unfriendly way, and a blank-faced official seated at a white table with a computer on it. Dhurgham told them who he was, his real name falling off his lips with a sweet sound and a bright inner pleasure. He stated that he was fourteen, from Iraq, and that he sought the protection of Australia from the certain horrible death that would await him in Iraq if he were returned; and he asked for their personal benevolence and indulgence in considering his youth and circumstances. He said he could see that they were men of honour and that Australia was a land of peace and happiness. He was glad they didn't ask many details, for he realised in that moment that he really didn't know anything about why it was dangerous for him in Iraq. He had heard many terrible stories from his fellow passengers and knew their reasons for fleeing, but had no idea about his own. He waffled vaguely about Saddam Hussein and, suddenly inspired by what others had told him, about the secret police. He was asked where his identity papers were and he told them he had left Iraq without them and then travelled on a false passport in a false name, a passport he threw overboard, as his travel agent had told him he should. The official was inscrutable. The translator sneered at him in a particularly Arab way and said something at the same time to the official. The official shrugged. A slim manila folder with his name on it was stamped; he was given the ID number RRN 230 and told to memorise it; and then he was in the searing and vapour-shaken heat of Florida Compound, the main part of the centre.

Dhurgham's donga could house sixteen but was less than half full when he moved in. Dhurgham was put in with the boys—rowdy, cheery, annoying boys, big and little. At first he was offended by their immaturity and then he found that the boys had a much better time than anyone else and he joined them.

He was at first delighted with the remoteness, secrecy and security of Mawirrigun. He felt an irrepressible happiness and his step had a spring to it. No doubt about it, this was a new opportunity for life. And the guards were mostly nice, especially once you got to know them.

He even prayed, feeling like a little kid. He had not prayed formally since leaving the mosque. Lots of people prayed, usually desperately, but Dhurgham prayed, smelling his clean palms, delighted. He felt special, chosen, saved even, and that was good cause to pray.

Mr Hosni would have a great deal of trouble finding him. Out in this red desert where he had a number, not a name! But he tried not to think about Mr Hosni. He liked the feel of the heat sizzling around him. He liked his thin warm brown arms and the red sand running between his fingers.

He was wary of men but befriended women and children in the centre easily. Many of the men here glowered with rage and shame, hopelessness and humiliation. They were strange and frightening to be around.

He quickly established that Nura, his mother and father were not there, and not known to have been there in the past. Mawirrigun was an old camp of some kind with new fencing and new demountables. Issam Dawsary and Julia Aquino, the oldest known inmates, had been there for eighteen months, and Julia said that they were with the first boatload to be imprisoned there. Dhurgham was jolted by the word prison; Julia was the first person he heard use it.

Dhurgham could not get to all compounds but nonetheless found out something of each of the seven hundred and fifty-four inmates who were not in initial processing in Vanuatu Compound. The centre was divided into seven compounds with the names of exotic holiday destinations. Some he had heard of: Hawaii, Fiji. Others, such as Vanuatu, Bali, were new to him. The main compound, Florida, had on the far side another small isolation compound named

Paradise, reserved for wrongdoers. He found out that Australia had eleven such centres but his hopes barely flickered. The country was not real to him. His family quickly faded again, present to him as a dreamy ache that he suppressed. Occasionally, when he felt bored and trapped, he put it down to the ache, not the wire, and he almost wished he were some precocious street child of Damascus—cheeky, nameless, stateless—survivor born free.

On his second day in the communal dongas after his interview, Dhurgham noticed a girl about his age with breasts. They were small, very pointed, round. They lifted her abaya, making it swirl around her belly, long legs and fine, dusty ankles. It had to be the breasts, for no other girl walked like that. He stared at her feet to avoid watching her breasts. He wandered back to his donga, thinking. That movement, that sway! He lay down on his bunk and recalled the image of her breasts again and again until he wore it out. 'Ma sha' Allah!' he said aloud, feeling the delight of a small transgression in even commenting on such beauty. Breasts! He felt as though he was the first person ever to notice them, ever to find such wonder and appreciation. They wobbled, firmly, softly. So round! He fingered his own nipple. Hers must be three times the size, at least, to be able to make the faint point in her abaya. And then his cock thickened and he stroked his hands down his bare belly, feeling himself rush through his skin and hands out to the tip of his taut penis. He touched it in delight. It was a sign. Here, all was right with the world. His body sang. His body was right.

Of course he would marry her. It would be difficult, as he had no parents to speak for him; but then, everything was different here.

He couldn't stand it any more. He leapt up to find her again.

He discovered that Thurayya Zahr lived with her mother and three other family groups in a donga four down from his. Thurayya! The name thrilled him. So fine sounding with his own. Dhurgham As-Samarra'i and Thurayya Zahr. She had a walk that made him dizzy.

After two weeks Thurayya stopped wearing her veil. She swayed around the compound with her mother, wearing the maddening abaya and a white embroidered hijab. Dhurgham followed her in an ecstasy of shyness and expectation until she turned around. She had a narrow face and huge dark eyes that for a moment Dhurgham thought unbearably beautiful. She looked him straight in the face and laughed.

'Mother-fucker,' she hissed. 'Cock-sucker. In your wildest dreams and then only my bum hole.'

• • •

His love for Laila Qahramani was of much longer duration. She was sixteen and Christian. Laila never affronted him. She didn't notice him. She could speak English and taught as a volunteer in the classes. The brush of her abaya on his forearm burned for hours. He would convert her, he thought. His steadfast punctuality and one hundred percent attendance in her classes would slowly attract her attention and she would see that he was a man of good character and decent aspirations.

His love for Laila only faded when he noticed Marwa. He had taken to staring surreptitiously at all the women and girls, studying them, trying to get a notion of their shape, their different forms, their breasts, necks, faces, legs. They were endlessly fascinating, endlessly different from each other. Marwa was just another object of fascination at first.

But Marwa became a friend, and his feelings about her body and his love became much more complicated. At the height of their friendship, he thought with some pride that he was really becoming a man, really learning to be responsible about passion. At the height of their friendship, he stopped staring at other women. He noticed them but without needing to divert himself all day with studying them.

Dhurgham noticed Marwa first because of her eyes. They were gazelle's eyes. Large, almond-shaped, black-rimmed. She was also tiny. She was about the size he was when he was maybe ten years old. And she had breasts—perfect, conical, pointy ones, with nipples pointing outwards. They were, suddenly, his favourite sort.

She was like a perfect miniature woman.

Marwa was dark and fiery. She spoke to him first, which shocked him. He didn't know that girls like her could do that. She was from Somalia but spoke perfect Arabic. 'I am as Arab as you are,' she said haughtily. She was pleased to tell him what an ignoramus he was about everything. Within two weeks they were as inseparable as they could be while flattering themselves that they were preserving the secrecy of their friendship.

Marwa and Dhurgham were behind the dongas, resting in the shade. It was a forty-nine degree day and everyone was inside, wilting under the fans while trying to keep small children and babies cool with wet cloths. The guards were nowhere to be seen—it was too hot for patrols.

The heat in the shade sizzled around Dhurgham. He said it was his halo. Marwa said it was his hell cloud. But it was almost too hot for talk and the walls were too thin to talk or shriek. Dhurgham twined Marwa's long sweaty fingers in his and leant back against the donga's stump. They had begun holding hands when no one was watching, outraging themselves at their own daring. They had begun competing for who could be the more daring lover, who could fly closest to the inferno of discovery, who could excite the other more.

Marwa pulled her hand away and faced him.

'You haven't done this before!' she whispered nervously, her eyes alight. She knelt in front of him, raised her hands, looked quickly along the deserted compound and took off her hijab. She shook out brilliant black curls, flowing from her high brow to her shoulders. With them wafted a perfume, the same as Dhurgham's shampoo, but somehow exotically different. She laughed nervously, breathlessly; she reached for his hand and placed it on her glittering hair.

He knelt facing Marwa knee to knee and stroked her hair in long wondering touches. He was shaking and dizzy. She closed her eyes and leant for a moment into his stroke. Her hair glittered with reflections of the red sand. Her hair made her cheeky face exquisite. This hot, shining hair was such a wonder! He felt as though the sand was rising under him like the waves of an ocean. He thought he might kiss her hair, kiss her.

Then fear overtook them both, fear of their own excitement and fear of discovery. Marwa, gasping, brushed his hands away, slipped on her hijab with trembling fingers and, with one laughing slap, ran out of their shady zone into the glaring white light. Then she was gone.

Dhurgham stared up at the burning blue. How would they manage to marry, here? They just had to. No matter what.

· · ·

Marwa's family got their visas. Marwa found out at two-thirty on Thursday afternoon and had ten minutes to pack and get on the bus. They weren't allowed to say goodbye to anyone properly. Marwa ran to the fence, in front of her mother and father and brothers, and touched Dhurgham's fingers through the wire. 'I'll write!' she whispered. She looked utterly happy and Dhurgham was bewildered. For a month with Marwa, he had thought that Mawirrigun was the best place in the world.

He wandered back to his donga. All Marwa's words seemed more real and meaningful now she was gone. Of course—how would she study to be a doctor like her father if she lived forever in prison? How would she raise children with him if she couldn't even teach them how to cook? He wondered for the first time what it was like in Marwa's donga. She had once said how embarrassing it was to have unrelated unmarried men sleeping in the same room as her and her mother, but she had never said anything about her parents except how stressed they were. They would have been stressed, waiting for their smart daughter to get on with her education. He had forgotten all about his own visa but of course Marwa hadn't forgotten hers. He knew that. He had just never thought about it. He tried to be happy for her and tried to imagine the Australian house they would have, its kitchen, bedrooms, living room. Verandah. He knew all the parts of a house from Australian culture classes, but he still couldn't imagine it and gave up. He felt lonely. He wondered for the first time what his chances of getting a visa really were. He had been here for four months. He certainly hadn't had a story like Marwa's to tell. All blood and gore and arson and attacks in the night. Lots of dead relatives. He had made his story up, for that matter.

He had a vivid picture of her running towards the shocked faces of her parents with her hand up both to reassure them and to farewell him, her abaya billowing and fluttering around her body, her hair bouncing under her hijab. Then Marwa running up the darkened steps of the open bus and its door hissing shut.

Dhurgham never received a letter from Marwa. There seemed to be a profound gulf between those who were released and those left behind. He felt as though he was in limbo in her past—she could no more have sent a letter than she could have travelled through time.

But Marwa did write. An AID officer wrote *Return to loser* on the envelope and posted it back.

Dhurgham's days after Marwa left were blank and boring. He took a while to get back to watching girls and women with any fervour, as it was such a small stimulation compared with Marwa. And he missed her—her face, her voice and her conversation. Her pinches and slaps. He was bored and cranky.

He picked his first real fight with a guard. He did it on purpose.

It felt really good.

He wasn't sure what he would do. He walked up to one of the new guards, a burly blond young man with spiked hair and black eyebrows who had been strutting back and forth in an annoyingly over alert manner; and then it came to him.

'Eh, Ustrali,' he said. 'When I get out I fuck your sister.'

The guard looked young and shocked for a moment, then reacted, to Dhurgham's surprise and strange pleasure, exactly as a boy on the streets of Damascus would have. He leant in quickly with one clenched fist up by his ear and shoved Dhurgham hard in the chest. As Dhurgham staggered back, the guard punched him, not particularly hard, in the face. Dhurgham reeled, but punched back with flailing, joyous arms, his muscles singing with the release of it. It was the two of them, in contest, adversaries. He felt a great appreciation for the blond boy, and tried, hopping around, to land him a good one. 'Filthy sand nigger,' the guard spat, breathing hard. Dhurgham was aware of guards closing in fast. He had to land just one and they would be equals. The guard blocked a snaking uppercut and then a baton came down and missed. Dhurgham hooked him on the cheek as some other

87

baton hit. He went down flailing as five guards filled his vision. He punched and writhed and kicked, laughing and half sobbing as they beat him down. He caught a glance of the blond guard, standing back as the more experienced men took over. The look on the young guard's face spoilt his pleasure a bit. The boy was holding his cheek, but the look on his face as he stared at Dhurgham was as one might look at a snake. Fascination, and disgust.

Dhurgham lay awake in a solitary cell in Paradise, feeling calm. It would have been better to have seen respect in that guard's face rather than disgust. But it had felt good to punch him. He sighed and sank into a dreamless sleep.

FILE NOTE
RRN 230, UAM, centre of disturbance approx.
1600 PM, 17 July 2000. Punched Officer Doyle
with witnesses in Florida. Officers Terrill and
Sexton corroborate Doyle's account that Doyle
struck first after verbal provocation. No charges
laid by either party.

Dhurgham began to wander around the compound at night in between head counts. Night-time was fascinating. The first time he went out to the perimeter fence at night he screamed when he startled three kangaroos in the starlight. But kangaroos, out there in the unreal world beyond the fences, were alien, and ultimately uninteresting. It was not as though he could get out and chase them. He turned his attention inward, to the known weird rub of the world, to the unhappy compound. He avoided the loud sobbing and the misery of domestic arguments that rang out from dongas here and there; rather, he sought out the electric charge that was all around, flickering from donga to donga, embracing guards and inmates alike. He saw men and women meet and whisper; he sprung other children spying on adults kissing; he heard the rustle, the urgency and the moaning of the charged darkness around the laundry; and he listened gleefully to the amplified chatter on the guards' radio trans-mitters. Night-time dissolved the fences and put him and the guards into an exciting, fantastical conflict, played out on a battleground of dangerous love and lust. He both spied on lovers and protected them. He distracted guards until shadows had parted. He imag-ined the guards with guns, hunting him; then he imagined himself with a weapon, picking them off when they least expected it. He flitted from shadowed donga to shadowed donga. He threw himself flat as deadly torchlight split the darkness. He was the tribal leader, conducting a one-man guerrilla war, giving his enemies the impression that he alone represented at least one hundred men. He was the sole surviving officer of the Republican Guard. He was selflessly throwing down his life for the pure loves of Qays and Layla, for Romeo and Juliet, for Mrs Azadeh and Abu Nizar.

When this game lost its excitement, which was usually when he found himself despising the lovers, lightly goading guards took over. He would hover where they might notice him. He stared guards down who hassled him to go to bed and laughed when they swore at him. He was a UAM—Unaccompanied Minor. They weren't allowed to touch him. All they could do was follow him around getting more and more huffy and saying nastier and nastier things.

He felt a bit sorry for them but that didn't stop him.

He sat on the stairs of the demountable and stared up at the desert stars. The brilliant spangle arched above him, as if glistening wet and phosphorescent. They looked so remote, so lost to him. He was not alien— this place was, even the stars. Then he found the cross, high in the sky rather than on the horizon. It was, after all, the same sky. He almost felt that he was looking into his past, looking at the stars, mapping something that can never again be. He suddenly recalled watching a faded film of himself as a toddler playing at the edge of the Southern Marshes, but he could not recall what it had been like, that sunny, humid holiday. He could not remember the taste or smell or feel of the reed pillars in the marshland houses, or the smell of the cows' breath. He could only watch himself enjoying them, on a flickering film fading against the night sky. It was as if that land, Iraq, was a land made up, put together soundless, without smell, out of snippets of other places.

If I were a bird, he thought, staring at the glitter of the universe above the camp, *they could not imprison me. Their luck and our misfortune that we are not birds.*

AID INTERVIEW REPORT
RRN 230, unaccompanied minor, claims to be an
Iraqi national, arrived unauthorised with no
papers 28 November 1999. Claimed to be aged
fourteen.
 When questioned in initial interview,
applicant at first claimed that he had no family.
Later he amended this and claimed that he had
last seen his family in Iraq but believed that they
did not want to see him, that they were
ashamed of him, that they were scattered in
Syria, Indonesia and even in processing centres
in Australia. When asked if he had relatives
living now in Iraq, said he did not think so
and that they all left at the same time. When
asked how many people all of his family
represented, he answered sixteen but on
questioning would not name his immediate family
other than repeating the surname he claims is his.

The interviewer at that time recorded that the applicant was extremely uncomfortable and answered with reluctance.

His claims regarding his departure from Baghdad are pure fantasy. He claims that the family, fifteen of them, crossed certain marshes, in April 1997. He does not recall the date. These marshes could not be near the border, which according to DFAT country information is all desert or saltpans, although the applicant claimed they were 'quite near'. He also claims now that they were 'near Baghdad' and that he can't remember how long it took to get there. He claims that he was asleep when they crossed the border and so doesn't know where or how they crossed. He also says that he went to Syria alone.

Summarising his claims is difficult, as they are so inconsistent. There is nothing in his story that hints at a believable escape route from Baghdad. It is not possible to believe the applicant's testimony, even with the most generous interpretation of the facts as he states them. There is no detail to his story. The above is all he would say.

Despite what he said in his initial screening interview he now states that he believes his family are all dead, killed in Iraq. When asked if he had ever been imprisoned he said no, he was only twelve when he left. When asked if members of his family had been imprisoned, however, he also said no. When asked why he believed his family had been killed he said that they all fled together.

According to his testimony, he was instructed by his father to not let anyone know that money was hidden in the lining of his clothes. They left the Karrada district of Baghdad at night, taking nothing with them. He claims that the entire extended family left in the same night. He claims he does not know why.

Claims that he was in Damascus for two years, helped by 'friends' not family. All further questions about his family and friends received vague or repetitive answers. When asked if there were any living members of his family or friends who could corroborate his story, he said he didn't know. When pressed about the friends in Damascus, he said they were friends to whom he 'paid money'. When asked where he got money, he said from his clothes. He flew from Damascus to Jakarta using this same money, helped by his friends, who took care of sourcing a people smuggler and making all transactions. He claims that he fled because his friends told him that 'bad Iraqi people' were after him and knew who and where he was, even though, as he himself says, he never used his real name in Damascus.

Needless to say I find much if not all of the applicant's story not credible. I do not find it convincing that the applicant lived from age twelve to fourteen off money he carried out of Iraq on his person, or that he lived away from his family with the help of 'friends' whom he paid. The applicant's claims about how, why and where he left Iraq are vague and inconsistent, and the information he provides about his family is unclear. The account is also not consistent with DFAT information on the region. A marsh crossing internal to the country itself is purposeless and unlikely, and he has nothing at all to say about how he got from there into Syria. I find these marshes to be a transparent fabrication and that the applicant most likely left Iraq in a completely different manner, or in fact knows nothing of Iraq at all and has made a story out of second-hand exit stories to Iran, not Syria. His only reason for such a fabrication would be to cover up a legal exit and make a false claim for refugee status or a false claim of nationality. If his family were indeed Iraqi, they had not, by his testimony, suffered persecution, and so should have been able to leave Iraq through normal channels; and, if they left legally and openly, there is nothing stopping them returning.

His account of his departure from Syria is concocted nonsense. He may well be lying in this instance to protect the identities of criminals.

Finally, I do not accept the applicant is fourteen, or that he was twelve when he left Iraq. He is well grown and unusually tall for an Iraqi fourteen year old. He could be as old as eighteen and, given that he has lied about other matters, I see no reason to accept that he is a minor and am compelled to see his stated age as another instance of an attempt to manipulate the system. A bone scan has not been undertaken but could settle the issue of age.

It is my view that the applicant, if he ever was in Iraq, left Iraq legally with his family along an ordinary route, and that he has reasons of his own for disconnecting from all who could verify his identity, if in fact he is who he claims to be, on which point there can be considerable doubt. He was evasive and extremely agitated in interview. As I find that he was not an illegal in Syria, the question as to whether he had effective protection in Syria does not arise, nor would return to either Syria or Iraq constitute refoulement in Convention terms.

The possibility remains that this applicant is a Syrian national with a poorly concocted story. The applicant provides no detail of his life in Iraq. By contrast, his life in Syria is rich in detail and clearly reflects lived experience. Intel that Iraqi *nationals seek protection more successfully in western countries than other Middle Eastern nationalities at the present time is readily available. The language analysis notes that he uses many Syrian words and phrases and that he has had a good education, which in Arabic can mask local region indicators. The language analysis was inconclusive, and doubt must remain as to whether he is Iraqi or Syrian. I note this for the record.*

I find that Australia does not have protection obligations under the 1951 Convention in this case.

Florida and Hawaii were in an uproar. Angry men and women shouted and waved their arms helplessly as heavily kitted guards held them back. Donga by donga, all their belongings were searched and anything suspicious confiscated. A knife had gone missing from the mess hall. Dhurgham was bundled out of bed and down the steps to wait with everyone else while all their things were thrown into the middle of each room. Nearly every donga had small souvenirs—food stores, cups, forks, spoons and home-made washing vessels, some fashioned from plastic bottles or even cartons. Guards who just half an hour before had chatted in a friendly way in the mess hall glared at them all and took everything, shouting out their disgust and crowing over finds, while the helpless men and women growled and yelled in impotent rage.

'Bloody thieving goat herders!'

'The filthy fuckers—look at this!'

'The bleedin' hearts oughta see this—'

'Phuuoh—the smell in here!'

The vessels attracted the most attention. Guards emerged carrying them at a distance between thumb and forefinger. The anger rose from a rumble to a cacophony of open shouting from the men around Dhurgham. A few voices managed to make themselves heard, first in Arabic and Dari:

'Where are you from, you no-brains, no-manners?'

'Where is freedom?'

'Shame on you, shame on your families!'

'Ignorant thieves!'

Then, in broken English:

'Wash! Clean! Need for clean!'

Officer Terrill held up his hand from the steps of Dhurgham's donga.

'You are in Australia now,' he said. 'Old habits die hard but you are in a civilised country now and can't do this sort of thing.'

'Fucken use toilet paper!' shouted a guard beside him. 'Disgusting!'

The vessels were all thrown with a pantomime of distaste into a garbage bag.

A battle raged between guards and inmates over washing vessels in the first six months of Dhurgham's incarceration. After a while there were 'toilet training' raids on any pretext and the guards conducted them more and more heavily armoured as the fury of the inmates increased to a mob roar. Guards made rude comments about Muslim toilet habits whenever they could be overheard (and regardless of whether their listeners were Muslim or not) and a trio of young Muslim men went out of their way to hover close and threaten guards with death and dismemberment. The older Muslim inmates finally managed to send a delegation to Mr Jensen, the centre manager. And then the whole thing faded: people kept and used their washing vessels unhindered, the strange became familiar to the guards and general staff and it was forgotten. Mawirrigun was like that.

Dhurgham was moved into Hawaii Compound. Hawaii was for those who were not expected to be accepted and its atmosphere was tense and strange at first. Hawaii was a brand on you, a statement about your worthiness and your prospects. You were shown up to all the others as one of the rejects.

'Now you are a refusee,' the grinning young guard said as he escorted Dhurgham to his new donga.

Dhurgham looked darkly at him. He understood, but the guard took his look to mean incomprehension. The guard rolled his eyes upward. He gestured elaborately at Florida. 'Refugees,' he said slowly. He then bowed to Dhurgham, and gestured as if flicking something from his fingers at Hawaii and said very slowly, 'Refusees.'

Dhurgham reddened and couldn't think of anything to say.

'Fuck you,' he said after a pause.

In Hawaii he was marked down as eighteen years old and housed with the men, not the unaccompanied minors. People in Hawaii sometimes got visas after their appeals, so they were better off than those long-term in Vanuatu, who had been screened out on arrival. But this added to the unusual tension of Hawaii. They had little hope, but some hope made life agony. A second fence covered in hessian was erected to prevent easy discussion through the fence between Vanuatu and Hawaii compounds. A riot in Vanuatu was triggered, guards said, by Hawaii inmates telling those in Vanuatu what their rights were and what they should have said at first interview.

The communal rooms in Florida had had posters of surf waves and palm trees on the walls. In Hawaii there was nothing.

Florida Compound had been ruled by waiting, by hope and expectation: Hawaii was ruled by rumour.

• • •

What Dhurgham liked about Hawaii in the first week was that he was free of the boys' silliness. And he loved that he was treated as a man. He was mustered and hassled and shouted at and befriended all as though he was eighteen or more, and he was hugely flattered. He was uncomfortable in his donga because of the slightly frightening press of men all around, but that didn't dim his spirits during daytime. Slowly, after the first month, he got to know them and to privately rank them for their harmlessness or otherwise. They were all Iraqi: Sunni, Shia and Kurd; several, like him, a mix of all three. He found that in Hawaii, Iranians, Iraqis and Afghans were generally separated from each other into discrete autonomous groups of demountables. Sabaeans were placed in a separate compound altogether. There was too much anger, too many recriminations and ultimately too many fights. Many guards were dismissive and hostile, but a few of the inmates were more scary, made worse by the fact that they could speak three or four languages, and could usually find a shared language through which to torment, frighten and humiliate others.

The men smelt bad. Some groaned all night and one ground his teeth. Some wandered in and out. Some cried or moaned and made him think uncomfortably about Mr Hosni. He found it hard to sleep.

He was relieved when Aziz, one of the UAMs from his former home, was rejected a month after him and moved into the bunk below him. They talked as if they were meeting for the first time.

Hawaii was not so crowded when Dhurgham was moved there. Not many had been rejected. Aziz had only been rejected because they had mixed up his case file with another, and had found his story to be bizarrely inconsistent. His lawyer told him not to worry about it. Aziz told Dhurgham, laughing nervously, that the interviewer had thought he was a Kurd with five children. He played with the idea, jokingly inventing names for his five daughters, praying loudly for a son. He patted his genitals, remonstrating with them, 'A son, is that too much to ask?' while Dhurgham rolled on the floor, crying from laughter.

Aziz wasn't afraid of the men in their donga and bit by bit Dhurgham got to know them through him. They stopped being a threatening conglomerate and became individuals. Abu Nizar, the quiet little man from Egypt who had been in Florida in the donga next to the boys, was his favourite. Al Haj, who smiled in the wrong way at the wrong times, was the one he feared and hated.

There were no girls in Hawaii yet. Only Mrs Azadeh, who was thirty-one and so didn't count. Both Dhurgham and Aziz were bitterly disappointed at this and kept praying that various girls from Florida and Vanuatu would make it to Hawaii. They spent happy hours inventing the many ways Mariam, Suzy, Shadia, Haifa, Sahar, Phuong or Lucia might fail dismally in their interviews. They giggled together delightedly. They saw themselves as the potential cheer to be offered the downcast and humbled girls.

The lack of women and girls drove all the men and boys closer to each other and for a while story-telling became the major pastime.

While in Hawaii Dhurgham learned of an Iraq he had never known or imagined. He carried with him a happy impression, the warmth of his mother, father and Nura, the atmosphere of singing to Beloved Uncle Abu Uday in school, but no sensual or even seemingly real memories. It was as if, in leaving, his memory had shut Iraq away from him and left him with only moods.

The Iraq he could barely remember was not a place of fear.

Nothing anyone told him gave him back the land, the city, the feelings he had known. Their Iraq reached out a terrible shadow over him, until their stories, vivid and horrible, came to meet him whenever he tried to remember. The people he was with, including seventeen year old Aziz, had stories of such grimness and such loss that his own absent narrative seemed a mere myth, misty, evanescent and mutable. It was not possible that his family was dead the way theirs were. Death was so major, so terrible, so violent, that one would know of it. It could not have taken place surreptitiously, behind your back, in a split second in the dark. He was reassured, oddly, by their stories. His could not possibly be as bad, or he would know.

Mrs Azadeh asked him, too, what had happened.

'I don't know,' he said softly and said no more. He smiled. In that moment he was sure they were alive. Mrs Azadeh hugged him, and for once he didn't mind that he was not really a man to her. In a strange way her hug confirmed his impression. It was a hug to tie him through until he was in a real mother's hug.

By cheek and good spirits, Dhurgham softened the guards, making them laugh when they least expected it. He discovered that they were, after all, quite different, each from the other. The younger Australian boys were easy to befriend: their aggression was bravado and their training recent, and Dhurgham instinctively saw through it. Some of the women were hard, always aggressive, and some of the men dangerous. But most softened for a time and even became friendly, especially if they were alone. This was before the centre filled beyond capacity and the stress of thousands of unhappy people set everyone on edge, made all programs in the centre impossible to manage, and frayed all tolerance.

And friendships with guards were fragile, especially in Hawaii. The constant insults and humiliation wore people's spirits: one only had to have a bad day, and snap or not smile, and the guards would feel that their friendliness was betrayed and would redouble the insults and indignities, not realising that the pleasantries, antics or forced friendliness of a captive to a captor can never dissolve the wrong of their relationship, or heal the damage done by abuse. The older guards felt that their extended hand was spurned by the fickle moods of their captives, that these people could not be trusted, and they became more certain in their distaste for their captives than if they had remained detached and encouraged no conversation, as their training instructed.

Mr Peter was no guard. He was the director of the education facilities. He was the nicest man in Australia—in fact probably in the world, Aziz said, as he was also the nicest man in Hawaii, Vanuatu, Bali, Florida. In fact, he was also the closest to God, Dhurgham added, as he was also the nicest man in Paradise, the isolation block. The two boys giggled until everyone frowned at them.

Mr Peter was much loved by everyone. Two of the new babies, born in the centre over the course of the year, were named after him. Peter Mohammad and Peter Muhsin.

Mr Peter ran a class for the older boys and young men that dealt with job applications in Australia. Even though they were refusees, many in Hawaii would get visas on appeal. These classes were run at Mr Peter's insistence, as they had a calming effect on the men as a group.

'You will need a resume, or curriculum vitae,' he

told them. 'This will tell your employer everything about you that he or she needs to know. Don't assume an Australian employer will automatically understand the education system or even the naming system in your country. You will need to provide some explanations. Tell them a little bit about yourself too, don't be shy.'

The interpreter, Issam Dawsary, who was also taking the class with them, turned in his chair and translated in three languages for those whose English was still weak. They could write in Arabic or Farsi or Dari first, then get help in translating it into English.

Mr Peter asked them to write first everything they could under the headings he gave them: Personal Details, Education and Training, Work Experience, Skills, Interests, Hopes and Ambitions.

Dhurgham looked at the headings in dismay. His was finished in a few minutes. He wrote his CV in Arabic and then on a new page in English. In English it was even shorter than in Arabic. Abu Nizar sitting next to him was writing page after page in deep concentration. Dhurgham's life added up to very little. He hung his head over his page, reddening. Mr Peter strolled by. He put his hand on Dhurgham's shoulder and pointed to the half-filled page.

'That is because you are very young,' he said. 'You fill it as you get older. You have beautiful hand-writing—you should mention that you are a talented artist.'

Dhurgham's shame receded, and he wrote, *I am a talented artist.*

Abu Nizar was still writing furiously. Dhurgham began to read over his shoulder. Abu Nizar's CV was the most beautiful anyone wrote that day.

Curriculum Vitae and Resume

Personal details:

Full Name: Ahmad Hassan Abdul Samit al Salih. Known as Abu Nizar after my son. It means Father of Nizar.

My First Name: Ahmad. My Middle Name: Hassan Abdul Samit. My Last Name: al Salih. My nickname: Abu Nizar.

My Date of Birth: 21 August 1964, a Tuesday, at midday.

My Place of Birth: Byala City, Kafr al Shaykh Governorate, Republic of Egypt.

My Gender: Straight Male, Non Smoker, Non Drinker, I do not wear any Glasses. 173 cm (5 feet 8 inches) 79 kilos (174 Pounds) foot wear size 44 European, light brown skin, black hair, brown eyes. I am widower, my wife died in 1987. I have a son Nizar Ahmad Hassan Abdul Samit al Salih, born 3 March 1986. God-willing I will marry again soon and live decently. I have two brothers, two sisters and I'm the eldest. I'm a Liberal, Open Minded Muslim.

Nationality: My Only Native Nationality is Egyptian. My Egyptian National Identification (ID) Number: 3 24 978 056 01 737.

Education: I am very well-educated. I am a man of the world, not just of Egypt, thanks to my parents, who supported me in everything, no matter the hardship to themselves. I have Elementary, Primary, Secondary Certificates and a University Degree. I have a Bachelor of Arts from the Cairo University, Egypt. I learned to love, not to hate.

Work Experience: My Egyptian Company for Trade and Repair Watches Licence Number 1024 with Shirbin City Council, Al Dakahlia Governorate, Arab Republic of Egypt, and that means that I'm horologist.

Skills: Mending Watches, horology and My Native Language is Arabic, English is my second language, and I love learning.

Interests: My interests are many. I love Honesty, Clearness, Transparency, Sincerity, Accuracy—as I'm horologist I see time as Gold. I want to learn languages in Australia, do bushwalk, build, think. I love Peace.

Hopes: I hope to join any job suits me as a Native Arabic Speaker, or mending Watches, I hope to be in good health, to help in making Peace in every place I'll be, and I hope that Peace be all over the world and violence, Wars stop all over the world, I hope that full mutual understanding become a reality in the world.

References: My Mother and Father and Brothers and Sisters can speak for me and my good bodily health and moral being. My trust too in God is complete.

Dhurgham had never guessed there was so much to meek Abu Nizar. Abu Nizar was no doctor, professor, minister or pilot. These were the jobs Dhurgham generally thought of when he thought of educated people. He had written them himself under 'Hopes'. Abu Nizar was a peace-loving horologist who was firmly anchored in place in the world. Abu Nizar could even remember his ID number and his business registration number off by heart. Australia would welcome such a solid, gentle man. Abu Nizar was what every employer would want. He looked down at his own life laid out in double-spaced blue pen on half a page. How could he compete with an educated horologist?

Dhurgham lay awake on his bunk. The heat was stifling, making it hard to breathe. Life would be easier if the donga was more crowded. He avoided looking across at al Haj. He knew that he would see two points glimmering in the darkness, swinging to meet his gaze, watching his every move. He was waiting for al Haj to sigh, groan deeply and turn to the wall. Until then, he wouldn't look that way. He hoped they wouldn't be left as just four in the room. With Mr Maamer gone (to prison, some said), Mr Mahmoud and Mr Bassam transferred, and Mr Hussein probably deported, the room was too empty with just four. Mostly it was just three, like now, because Abu Nizar went for long walks out in the starlit compound, looking for constellations and probably for Mrs Azadeh. The worst would be if Aziz were given a visa before another boatload arrived and made it to Hawaii. Aziz below him was breathing heavily, quickly, in the darkness. They probably had two hours before the guard came by for headcount. Dhurgham wanted to hit Aziz. He imagined leaping off the bunk and ripping the skinny body off the sweaty bed below, throwing him to the floor and kicking, kicking, kicking. He tensed, as if to leap, but just exhaled his strange fury at the ceiling. The fan went round and round, gleaming in the shadow. On and on without effect. He wanted to throw something at the fan, leap up and in the darkness, bend, break its arms and make its slow circling twisted, broken. Round and round, but idle. A slight whispering creak repeated over and over again. The bunk began to rock slightly in rhythm with the fan. Dhurgham stared more peacefully, rocking too with the fan, deliberately rocking Aziz below him. He found himself tuning in with the urgent rhythm beneath, and rocked Aziz to the end. He often despised Aziz these days but if tonight Aziz had offered to touch him in the darkness, he would have stared at the fan and almost gratefully let him. But Aziz stayed where he was, locked in his private cradle.

Dhurgham felt like crying, he was so lonely. He heard al Haj smiling or grimacing through a sigh in the dark.

One morning Dhurgham woke up and wanted his freedom. He wanted to be out and away from the wire and the red earth and never see them again. He wondered briefly whether they would just let him go if he pleaded eloquently enough. He didn't think Mr Chris was a bad man, just a man with a difficult job. Mr Peter had told him so many times. He didn't like to think about it, but he had a lot of money in his belongings. Mr Hosni's money would pay for it. He would tell them, it's OK. I'll leave here and go somewhere else. I'll go to … Africa. Or Sweden. He wondered whether he should do something with lawyers. It couldn't be that he was supposed to stay here for the rest of his life. It couldn't possibly be what they intended.

He wanted to see Mr Chris.

Dhurgham had never been in the centre manager's office. He was surprised by its settled, civilised feel. It gave a sense of being a permanent space, in which a work life took place, day in day out, a space ornamented with personal belongings, but with no air of impermanence or desperate clinging. It was as though Mr Chris's office were in another country. He sat down with Mr Peter in matching blue cloth armchairs. Only the red desert and stumpy casuarinas outside the window placed this office in the world of the centre. Three different photos of a beautiful golden haired woman and two teenage children about Dhurgham's age stood on the desk, and Dhurgham wondered whether Mr Chris missed them.

Chris Jensen had until this point barely noticed Dhurgham. There were a lot of dark-haired, dark-eyed swarthy boys in the centre. There were more than eighty who looked pretty much the same. Dhurgham stood out only because he was tall. The faces blurred into one another.

But anyone who proposed to drop their protection claim and to volunteer to return was different.

He saw a thin boy of perhaps fifteen. Strikingly tall. That was his first impression. And, separated from the rest, it was a distinctive face. Beautiful, angular, slightly fierce. But the boy's proposal was naïve and preposterous. Mr Jensen rested his hands on the desk and flashed Peter an annoyed glance. Peter should have known better, really, and counselled the boy without bothering him.

'You know we can't just send you off to any country,' he said kindly. 'We have to find one that will have you first, or wait and see whether something changes in Iraq and makes it possible to send you back home.'

The boy flushed. 'I have money,' he said softly.

'Well, that's not a solution to everything,' Mr Jensen said coldly. 'Being locked up here should make that clear to you.'

The boy stood up and bowed with otherworldly courtesy, hand on his heart.

'You try to help me,' he said through suddenly pale lips, and Mr Jensen was unsure whether it was an exhortation or irony, or just a formal thank you. He sighed. The phone rang and he reached for it, relieved, waving to Peter and Dhurgham to go.

From that day on Dhurgham saw his imprisonment differently. The idea that it would be hard to find a country that might want him rang on as a discovery, an awful one. It had never occurred to him how little he might matter. He lay awake that night in his bed, feeling diminished. Even to Mr Hosni he had been special, wanted. He wondered with a rising unease whether it was true that all the boys like him were just so much unwanted refuse. All the lost boys hugged by the sailors on the great ship, wrapped around with blankets, spoon-fed by gentle hands, meaning ... nothing. Tears seeped from his closed eyes. You needed parents, you really did. You needed a sister. His self-pity calmed him and moved him to new vistas. *It is good*, he thought, *that I can weep for myself. A very good sign.* Then he opened his eyes; he was sure, now, that he simply had to find them, even if it took his whole life. And he would love himself as much as possible to keep himself whole until they could take over again. He would get out and find Marwa and she would help. Then he fell asleep.

The boredom of every day dragged at him and the hours scraped away his good spirits. He had too much time. Time to kick sand at the sky. Time to scratch the paint off the wall by his bed; time to chew his fingernails off; time to pick holes in himself fossicking for nonexistent pimples and time to pick endlessly at the scabs; time to goad and annoy other people; time to think.

He sat on the steps of his donga watching others play soccer. Three little girls whose names Dhurgham couldn't remember walked purposefully up to an unfamiliar officer who was standing legs apart, hands clasped behind him, eyes on the middle distance: the distinctive over alert pose of the very new. They looked out sideways from their hijabs at him and swung their bodies side to side, hands clasped behind their backs.

'Hello Officer!' the oldest said.

'Hello Officer!' chimed the younger two.

'Hello little girls,' he said, leaning down, smiling. 'Don't you look nice today!'

'Fuck you, Officer!' all three shrieked and ran away laughing. 'Fuck Australia!'

Dhurgham smiled nastily.

'Why do Australians do this to us? We are not criminals.'
Aziz's voice had a panicked edge to it. Aziz, Dhurgham
and Abu Nizar were sitting in Mrs Azadeh's donga,
which she shared with another woman, Lina, and her
daughter Suha, and two other families. Suha was about
sixteen and very shy. She had large green eyes and, from
what Dhurgham could tell from the hair that fanned
like a bird's wing by her ear, she had fine black hair,
probably very long, as there was a bunch at the back of
her head.

It was a lovely donga. A fine red silk sari embroidered with gold thread, traded from someone, was
hung in carefully designed folds over the window, and
paintings done by the children in the art centre,
selected for their rich colours, were arranged above the
beds. There was even a painting done by Dhurgham
prominently hung. It was a portrait of Mr Peter and a
little girl who had long ago left the centre, laughing
together behind a mist of thrown red sand. A small
upturned box covered in blue velvet was the table for
a leather-bound Koran, a hand-carved water jug and
the fine scroll of a rolled prayer rug. Everyone liked
Mrs Azadeh's donga. Bunk beds were pushed to the far
wall and mattresses and pillows thrown down to create
a comfortable living room spacious enough for at least

twelve people to recline in a circle. And if her sessions went late into the night, the guards were lenient, at least for a while, and conducted headcounts in good spirit without making them get up and straighten the room.

Mrs Azadeh liked to invite Dhurgham and Aziz over with Abu Nizar as 'father' and to tell stories together. They told epic adventures of Salahuddin, Sayf bin dhi Yazan the Yemeni, and others. All popular, light stuff. And they told their own stories, the laughable and terrible things that had happened to them on their various journeys. They shared and laughed over anecdotes about their experiences in Mawirrigun: Dhurgham and Aziz drove adults crazy with giggling role play and re-enactments after Mrs Azadeh told them that for her first month in the centre she thought 'Fuck off' and 'Fuck you' were Australian courtesies.

But tonight Aziz's grim mood dominated, and his question hung in the air. Aziz's lawyer had said that he would be out as soon as his case was heard, but that had been four months before. The case was heard, Aziz won, but then nothing happened.

No one felt like telling stories tonight. Lina sighed.

'No one in Australia knows about what happens here. Until you are freed, you are not in Australia,' she said. 'My husband has been in Melbourne for a year. All the people, they are lovely. They gave him a mattress, a quilt and a computer and much more, and they help take our son to school every day.'

'They must know. They just hate us. They hate the Arabs. They blame us,' muttered Abu Nizar.

'We are not all Arabs here, and hate us for what?' Aziz was almost shouting. His young voice cracked into a squeaky sob.

'For all the unhappiness of the world. We are the new Jews.'

Dhurgham was silent. Even Suha's company across the room barely stirred him, even though, as everyone knew, she was the reason he and Aziz came so eagerly to these gatherings. He saw a tear on Suha's cheek, and still sat detached, even annoyed with her. He had heard the same kind of things over and over, the same despair, the same overwhelming reasons for every-thing, the same hope for the real Australia, and the same lugubrious resignation. It was all the same, every day. Yet just now he could dimly perceive that he and Aziz and the other lost boys were the pioneers in a new world, and that, really, it was up to them to stand up and be men and refuse this humiliation, shake it off. He wanted to strike Abu Nizar for his resignation.

He felt utterly depressed.

He felt like punching a hole in the thin wall. If Mr Hosni were to appear suddenly in Mawirrigun, he would leap upon him like a wild animal and beat him senseless. He hoped for Mr Hosni's appearance with a kind of thirst. And Mr Hosni, he was sure, had no idea what would await him if he travelled after Dhurgham to Australia. Humiliation, indefinite imprisonment and Dhurgham's revenge. And then he felt the cold sweat spring out on his back and throat with terror that Mr Hosni might appear, might twist him, take the upper hand. He focused on reconstructing those piles of money, stack by stack, slowly feeling into his child-memory for just how much money that had been. US dollars, in 100s; not riyals, or dinars or lira. It must have been—$500 000. It could not possibly have been spent in two years on rent and food and scouts. It would have paid the airfare, the expenses, Mr Leon's fee, and plenty to spare. He was an idiot baby, and he shuddered in his bunk with self-revulsion.

Dhurgham once made a small wooden horse and warrior for Mr Hosni. It took him three days. He had made them before, one for Nura first, then his uncle, then the best one for his father. But the one he made for Mr Hosni was the best of all, for it was so well balanced that it stood up, while the others had needed a ball of sticky tape under one hoof to counter the raised foreleg. It was glossy and smooth, round-muscled, proud-limbed, the warrior erect, with a scimitar in his hand. Mr Hosni had had tears in his eyes when he received it and had treasured it. Mr Hosni knew and appreciated the making of things. Dhurgham's father had not treasured his, and Dhurgham had kept it on his own windowsill for him. Dhurgham, staring at the ceiling from his bunk, saw himself fashioning the joints and the limbs of that horse, and he hated himself with a bitter violence, and hated Mr Hosni more. His face twisted, eyes looking at nothing, and he swore softly, over and over again, but he could get no relief. Aziz asked him what was happening, man, and he punched Aziz full in the mouth, then threw himself out of the door and into the dusty compound, speechless. He marched head down back and forth along the perimeter fence, swearing in English, 'Fuck shit fuck fuck fuck!'

He felt ashamed ten minutes later, but when he went back to apologise to Aziz, he felt like punching him again as soon as he saw him, so he stayed silent, climbed into his bunk and stared at the ceiling again.

Mr Hosni's voice crept back into his ears. He and Mr Hosni were watching TV, Mr Hosni raised an eyebrow at something and snorted in comical disbelief. He couldn't remember what it was. He could remember Mr Hosni's face and his own feelings. They laughed together until they cried, then sighed and ate.

Dhurgham began to weep with rage. A con man! A con man had taken his family's entire wealth. He suddenly leant over the side of the bunk and vomited onto the floor, making Aziz under him jump and swear.

'Are you sick?' Aziz asked, trying to break into Dhurgham's rage, seeking an apology.

Dhurgham didn't answer. He found himself, surprisingly, sobbing. Nooni would be such a beautiful woman now! He would be so proud of her. He longed for her with every muscle and every bone of his chest. *My sister sister sister, save me*, he whispered, and sobbed himself to sleep.

With a sister, with Nura by his side, he would have had proof that he was slotted in like a piece of the puzzle into the world. Without her, he had no home.

A Thursday came in which Aziz suddenly got his Permanent Protection Visa, became an Australian, and disappeared in a puff of crazy joy. Dhurgham missed him bitterly. He lived one week in sleepless fear of al Haj, and then, to his astonishment, al Haj got his visa too and was gone. Dhurgham slept for forty-eight hours and woke to find his donga had filled with strangers.

Abu Rafik had no son named Rafik. He was called that because of a small boy he had adopted, an orphan from Palestine. No one mistreated or yelled at Rafik because most were afraid of Abu Rafik's tongue. Everyone respected Abu Rafik, even when they resented him. Rafik disappeared one day, when Abu Rafik gave the guards a piece of his mind in broken English, and after that Abu Rafik became silent. Rumour spread that the guards had killed Rafik to break Abu Rafik's spirit and then buried his body out in the red sands where no one would ever find him, but a lawyer told Mrs Azadeh that Rafik had been moved to Kanugo Kagil, a processing centre in the city of Sydney.

The guards were mostly just teenagers themselves, and the older men and women found it hard to submit to their buttocks and calves being tapped and prodded by the batons of these boys, to having half-broken voices abuse them or humiliate them with petty rules. It didn't take anything too dramatic to break someone's spirit.

Abu Rafik ignored Dhurgham for a while and then began to watch him. Dhurgham felt the eyes of the old man on his back and developed an unreasoning fear of Abu Rafik's calm and silent face. Had Rafik been his lover? Was he looking for another? He gave the older man one or two filthy looks in the hope that this would put him off. He began to have nightmares that took him back to Damascus. He wished Aziz were still with him. Then he began to want Abu Rafik's glances because they gave him something and someone to hate, something to focus on. He started to think of insulting things he could say to the old man should he get up the courage, or should the old man try anything, anything at all. He imagined various forms of righteous violence against the vile old fellow, once all was revealed, and took to catching glimpses of Abu Rafik and muttering to himself darkly over him.

So one day when Abu Rafik sent for him, Dhurgham was very nervous, and ready to fight or bribe or abuse and shame the older man, anything. He was dizzy, walking on the balls of his feet, his mind racing.

Abu Rafik was kneeling on a prayer rug in the recreation room, staring at his hands, as if he had finished praying but could not return to action. His clothes were impeccably clean, unlike Dhurgham's which were stained with the red dust of the compound. Abu Rafik greeted him courteously and then waited a moment until the other men in the room had moved away. Then he said a shocking thing.

'I knew your father, ya Ibni.' His voice was very quiet. His accent was Syrian. He raised his eyes to Dhurgham's white face. Dhurgham stood, frozen, unable to bring his dream father into this world so quickly, unable to think, groping to find whether he should be happy and slip into decent manners, or be very afraid. The old, real world shuddered into being within him. His father. He was shaking, clammy, staring, and all the strange madness of the past Abu Rafik-hating weeks drifted away. He thought he might pass out.

Abu Rafik's face was open and calm. 'I was a friend,' he said even more softly, so only Dhurgham could hear, and Dhurgham sat down in front of him, his legs failing under him. And suddenly, as if an airhole at the end of a long darkened cave was opened, Dhurgham sensed rather than recognised that this man was familiar. He had a memory, buried somewhere, of this man.

'Where is he, Uncle?' he whispered through dry lips.

Abu Rafik's face clouded and Dhurgham saw him hesitate but didn't know how to read it.

'I don't know, my son,' Abu Rafik said slowly, barely audibly. 'No one has seen him since he, you, fled. Be careful, now. Don't look around. Even here there are eyes and ears.'

Dhurgham from then on clung to Abu Rafik, hardly allowing the older man breathing space. He never learned any more about what had happened to his family, but he learned a lot about himself and his father, about life and about Iraq. Abu Rafik became his teacher and Dhurgham's love of books and of knowledge resurfaced and took over his whole self. He felt as though the boy who had been switched off like a light at age twelve was suddenly switched on again, and he clutched at that confident and beloved former self. The intervening years seemed just a bad dream, something putrid and painful that he stored well wrapped up and almost forgotten among his things. With the return of his old self, a world unfolded as if shaken out and spread over everything, a world in which people discussed good and evil, right and wrong; in which one strove for the light; a world ordered by goodness, principles, teachings and wisdom flowing from fathers to sons.

But this was no return to the past. With this world came, finally, his grief, bringing back to him Nura's face, with all its mobility and fierce love. His mother's and then his father's. His memories overwhelmed him, leaving a mist only over the escape. After a week of daily lessons with Abu Rafik, Dhurgham asked him whether his father would really be so angry that he would not seek his son. Abu Rafik told him gently to study, now, in honour of their memory. And Dhurgham sobbed for an hour into the old man's chest under the watching eyes of the others and the gaze of the discomforted guards.

Abu Rafik started the next lesson differently.

'Recite the Fatiha,' he said gently.

Dhurgham recited the Fatiha.

Abu Rafik was silent for a moment. Dhurgham waited.

'All the Koran is contained in the Fatiha,' Abu Rafik said then. 'And all the Fatiha is contained in the bismillah at its beginning. All the bismillah is contained in the "b", and all the "b" in this one tiny dot.' He wrote the long boat of the letter 'b' on a piece of paper, adding its single dot last. 'The mystics would say, "I am the dot!"' Abu Rafik turned and looked at him. 'There is a whole universe inside you, Dhurgham.'

Tears burst from Dhurgham, this time for happiness. This was the truth he himself had glimpsed alone, in extremity on the ocean.

He felt loved. Discovered.

He could almost hear his mother's voice at night in the donga, breathy and gentle. He could see her face and hands as she packed the eggs she had just carried in from the nests under the palm grove. He saw her thin, bent back as she hoed with Ahmad under the palms, showing him how to do it. He could see her face, angular and worried. He could see her eyes, so like Nooni's, but with no fun in them. He could remember how annoyed he would get if she asked him to help Ahmad to change over the kerosene. He could remember her laughing, too, when he snuggled up next to her on the mattress on the roof as they all lay together and listened to the noises of sleepless Baghdad under the velvet sky, the city coming alive after the fierce heat of the day. How much they loved summer nights!

He remembered her hands turning the pages of his schoolbooks and her windy voice in his ear.

He was suddenly so rich in memories that they

seemed to tumble out of control and out of sequence as he tried to hold and hoard them.

He tried to honour his parents with everything he did. He became dogmatic and serious as he struggled with the living pull their loss now had on his body and mind. He studied the rush of memories he now had of his father, reeling in grief but thriving on it. His house and his childhood came back to him in full sound and colour, filled with their voices, their bodies. He could remember Ahmad and the narjeela workshop. He could hear and see how his father acted, spoke, interacted with others. He tried to use the same quiet voice, the same sideways tilt to the head, listening; he tried to quieten his limbs into an older man's step and school his mind to older men's higher purposes. He tried to avoid watching the girls and young women, schooling his passions, con-centrating on his sister, on her face, her arms, her laughter. He stopped visiting Mrs Azadeh and Suha, and the mothers and children, remembering that his father never played with children except diffidently; never played with Dhurgham except for a few delicious minutes while he drank coffee. Children came to his father, not the other way round. But the children didn't seek Dhurgham out, spooked by his new self, so he stopped playing altogether. He let his memory train and dominate him, needing his father but, as time went by, missing his sister more and more bitterly.

The others mistrusted Dhurgham's transformation, seeing it, rightly, as a performance, as somehow dissembling, and of course they preferred his former easy, charismatic charm or rowdy playfulness.

'Let him be,' Abu Rafik said quietly when they teased Dhurgham for what they called his fundamentalism. 'He is trying to please dead parents. It takes time.'

Dhurgham's stiffness, his unexplained internal protocols, were all blamed on Abu Rafik. Both inmates and AID staff watched the influential old man uneasily. The centre had swelled, rumoured now to house thousands, and tension flickered like lightning between them and across the compounds.

About this time, Abu Rafik, partly inspired by Dhurgham's intensity and partly grieving for all the bored and wasted boys and young men, did something that made perfect sense to him. He started an Islamic school. Only boys attended. He had not ever said anything against girls attending, but, when the boys took to the school with a kind of possessiveness, the girls sensed it and, under pressure of ridicule from their brothers and from the overwhelming numbers of boys there would have been to each girl, they stayed away. Dhurgham was pleased. Girls were a huge distraction.

At first only the teachers knew of Abu Rafik's school and treated it as an asset and a relief from their own impossible teaching loads. They knew the children and many of the young men, and liked Abu

Rafik, so the sight of several rows of unusually well groomed and cleanly dressed boys seated in front of Abu Rafik didn't at first bother them. Many of the guards, however, were deeply disturbed, particularly by the recitation in unison of the Koran by the frighteningly well-behaved group. To some of them Abu Rafik's class had the look of an army. They were disgusted and outraged that girls didn't attend.

Abu Rafik taught the Koran, Islamic history, literature and philosophy. Attendance was high and some boys began to practise recitation in meditative poses at times outside class. Within four weeks, what had started as a once a week event had become daily. On Fridays they did just Koran. Those members of the male population who had been branded as troublemakers had never been more quiet. The centre seemed to be running very smoothly, and Abu Rafik's class rose to over two hundred.

Dhurgham washed his clothes assiduously and carried himself with quiet pride. The highlight of his day was kneeling in that precise formation of men, watching the backs in front of him and to the sides, sensing the rustling, living whole behind him. He absorbed Abu Rafik's lessons with intense concentration and purpose. Prayer made him flood with grief and with openness, and, as he bent his face to the ground, he felt the tears rush unchecked. Poetry of heroism made him think of his father, and his heart swelled painfully with the glory and tragedy that his life would have to emulate. Death was not so bad a thing, he told himself, if you died well, if you died with nobility and as a great human being. He wept as he gloried in what he imagined to have been his father's story. He pieced together every tiny part, every word Ahmad had said, every word Abu Rafik had said, and he saw it all in shining legend. He imagined some terrible unequal battle in which his father's last stand became intertwined with the murder and martyrdom of Hussein at Karbala.

In moments of twilight, comforted by Abu Nizar now sleeping under him in Aziz's bunk, he found that there was no way his father could really be dead. The legend was about someone else, not his father.

It was one of the happiest times of Dhurgham's life. He felt manly and good, calm at heart. He loved calling Abu Rafik 'Ammu', Uncle. He loved it that Ammu called his father Abu Dhurgham. He felt himself slip into a proper place in the company of men. Mr Hosni vanished altogether for a time from his worries and his dreams. He felt how fine a thing it was that he was lucky enough to be born Arab and Muslim. He felt that he was catching at the shadow of his father, becoming everything he, Dhurgham, could be. He thought about the Great Mosque, about its history and its beauty, and he felt overwhelmed by the thought of such beauty. He studied hard, obsessively, determined to catch up with all he had lost. He concentrated on those philosophers and pieces of Islamic history he thought his father would have admired most. He was sure that his father's heroism and goodness could be transmitted through arcane and miraculous means if they touched each other through the same texts. Abu Rafik encouraged him to think like this; even, cautiously, occasionally revealing that he knew Abu Dhurgham had read this or that thinker.

The school had to be conducted in the open air within two months of its inception, late in the afternoons and early in the morning. Dhurgham's heart swelled with pride as he sat out in the red earth, surrounded by the shining fences. He felt the potency of patience steady him. He was glad that there was some vicissitude against which he could prove himself. He was glad there were fences. Abu Rafik took care to tell the stories of those imprisoned and how nobly they endured it.

Abu Rafik had a motley collection of Arabic books, and Mr Peter allowed him to keep them with him to prepare lessons. The Australian Arab Council for Culture and Community had donated a collection of hardcover books, including a number of Korans, and several sets or part sets of some of the great classics of Arabic literature: part of the twenty-five volume collection of the *Kitab al Aghani*, the complete four volume *Tales of the Arabs*, the *Maqamat* of al Hariri, some al Jahiz, half of al Tanukhi's *al Faraj ba'd al Shidda*, and Ibn Khaldoun's *Muqaddima*. Abu Rafik also had a prodigious memory and could recite innumerable poems from the great age of Arabic poetry. He could have taught on the Koran without a copy to hand.

Someone sent a detailed, highly critical description of Abu Rafik's school to AID in Canberra without consulting the Arabic interpreters or Mr Peter and the other teachers. The report included photos of rows and rows of mostly white-clad men and boys praying. But for the red sand and the dongas and razor wire, it could have been in Afghanistan. In the conclusion the report stated that the school had all the makings of a terrorist training camp, ironically fully funded by the Australian Government.

The school came to an abrupt end.

'You are a dangerous man,' Chris Jensen said to Abu Rafik in front of Dhurgham. 'One of those types who hype up suicide bombers with hashish and brainwashing talk. We won't be giving visas to men like you, that's for sure. If I see you with more than this puppy hanging off your words, I'll slap you in solitary faster than you can say AllaAkbar. And if there is a riot over this, I'll be blaming you.'

'If there is a riot, you will have caused it!' Dhurgham said, but he said the last two words in Arabic. Mr Chris looked at him coldly and Abu Rafik silenced him with an eyebrow.

• • •

Dhurgham was back to private lessons with Abu Rafik. The spell was broken and he struggled daily to find the peace and sad glory with which the school had filled him. He chafed at the lessons and sometimes would rather have been playing soccer with the other boys and young men.

'What would you like to be when you grow up?' Abu Rafik asked him one day at the end of the lesson.

'Free,' Dhurgham said. It wasn't even his answer— it was everyone's first thought. He had soaked it up from the atmosphere.

'You'll be free from here in five minutes, when the time comes. Just as in death, ya Ibni.'

Dhurgham didn't listen to the last part. He was thinking about the first. Being free was so easy, and so out of his control, that it obviously couldn't be a lifelong goal. 'Then, when I'm free, I want to fight,' he said, blushing as he searched for his war.

'Fight what?'

He couldn't say, *just fight.* 'Jihad. The Isra'ili,' he said.

'What do you know of jihad?' Abu Rafik was looking him firmly in the eye.

Dhurgham squirmed, then recited a line from the Koran in a faint voice.

Abu Rafik sighed. 'Tell me the meanings of the verb form jahada, other than to fight for something.'

'To endeavour, to strive, to struggle, to overwork ...' Dhurgham said.

'There are many ways to fight injustice. Your art can be jihad, ya Ibni.'

Dhurgham couldn't let the idea go. The idea of heroism, righteousness *and* the song in his body of destruction. He fantasised about killing all the guards, Mr Chris; how quickly and absolutely his wrath would come down upon them! In their shocked dying glances they would see that they had been wrong to misjudge him as a stripling, a weakling; to humiliate the men and women in front of him, to torment the defenceless children, to shut down the only good thing. He practised his moves in the donga. What strength these arms! This torso! If he saw Mr Hosni now, he would strike him down with one blow of his fist and khalas! all would be over and cleansed between them.

'Who took care of you in Syria?' Abu Rafik asked one day.

Dhurgham twisted in misery and was silent. Abu Rafik stared at him, silent too, until Dhurgham said, 'A man. Mr Hani Hosni,' and felt his throat tighten until no more sound could come out.

Abu Rafik was no fool. 'It is all closed now,' he said, and continued with the mathematics lesson.

But it was not closed. Dhurgham had shut that part of his life away, now, for months. But after the school closed Mr Hosni came back, agreeing in his soft voice, insisting: 'No, it is not closed, is it, Birdie?' He could not think of Mr Hosni's too-moist eyes and smooth face without feeling a wave of shame. Not for what Mr Hosni had done. No. Quite the reverse. Dhurgham would have given anything to undo their parting; to smile into the older man's eyes, to hold out his hand and to thank him in a considered but none-theless warm voice for all he had done. He writhed, thinking of his new clothes, his brand-new western backpack, his Nike sneakers. Dhurgham blushed a furious red every time he remembered the $10 000 US dollars he had found in his pack in Indonesia. Even though he knew it was his money, it was so shockingly generous, so unlike Mr Hosni not to have crowed about it. The money still lay untouched in its brown Syrian envelope in the centre somewhere with his name on it, with his belt and his gold chain, all presents from Mr Hosni.

Dhurgham cringed inside. Their parting loomed over him, increasing in proportion over time. He imagined again and again the hurt look he had not let himself take in and imagined with crawling horror a clinging Mr Hosni travelling to Australia to find him and exact absolution from him. *You have forgiven me, Birdie? Your old uncle? You've found another uncle to replace me, I see.*

Dhurgham had stood, face averted, and had said nothing. His skin had been shrinking away from Mr Hosni, from Syria, and he was impatient for his freedom, there waiting for him on the plane to Jakarta. He had wanted to hurt Mr Hosni. He had said nothing into the yawning, yearning silence between them. He had felt it pull with desperate fingers at his mouth and throat; yet, despite the pain of holding the words pent in his chest, he had said nothing. Nothing at all. The dialogue that should have been quietly closed in a manly way was left open, longing for repair. He felt the unspoken words and Mr Hosni haunting him, as if this, a moment of rejection of a *bad* man, was the worst crime, the thing his father would not have done, yet another thing he could not bear Abu Rafik to know about him. Deserting his family, leaving them destitute, seemed now less certain and accusing than this. He even wept over Mr Hosni and then raged at him, telling himself again and again that Mr Hosni was filth and should be killed.

ALIENS PROTECTION AUTHORITY: REVIEW HEARING.
… The applicant is clearly uncomfortable speaking about his family and completely unable to talk about what happened in the crossing from Iraq into Syria, which involved a marsh crossing and probably a journey by road, as indicated also in his AID interviews. I do not find his testimony weakened by this. He was twelve at the time and, although there is no psychological assessment on file, his discomfort and silence and, in earlier hearings,

evasiveness, can be explained as a reaction to trauma, which is at the least a reasonable assumption, given that no member of his family was with him in Syria or is contactable now.

I find it distasteful to suggest that a child of twelve was so deeply embroiled in crime that he has taken these lengths to bury a former identity when a simpler explanation stands out: the applicant lost his family and cannot speak about it. He was a child.

I questioned him about his evidence that his family had not suffered persecution, as is deduced from his first interview hearing. He said he was never asked this. I have checked the record and he is correct. He was asked if any member of his family had been imprisoned or tortured or killed. He said that his oldest cousin disappeared, simply did not come home from work one day, shortly before the two families left. He said that his father and his uncle did not show themselves on the street and stayed hidden in the family home for about a month before the family fled, and he was cautioned to say nothing at school, and to say, if asked, that his father was away in the south on business for some months and would return before Eid with presents. I find no reason to disbelieve this evidence. Persecution begins at some point. I accept that until shortly before they left, this family had probably not suffered significant persecution. I also accept that at age twelve, and the baby of the two combined families, the applicant would not have known why or known

all the background of his parents' concerns. I reiterate,
he was a child.

I find that he is a refugee for the purposes of the
1951 Convention vis-a-vis Iraq. It remains to be
determined whether he had effective protection in a
third country, in this instance Syria, where he lived for
two years under a false name. His evidence is that he
was taken in by what seems to have been a shady
character who charged him exorbitant prices but fed,
clothed and sheltered him, and, ultimately, for a fee,
put him in contact with a people smuggler and
arranged his trip to Indonesia and Australia.

From the description given of the family home in
Baghdad, this was a wealthy family. The language
assessment of the applicant's speech also suggests this.
He has had an education in a good urban primary
school, as he himself testifies. I do not, however, accept
that the applicant was able to secrete the money he
claims he was carrying and live off it for two years and
pay a people smuggler. From his evidence I believe he
worked in Syria. His evidence is that he did not: that
the only work he could have got would have been
'shameful work'. I believe he has made a story out of
his time in Syria that is more appealing to him than
his actual experiences there, but I do not find that this
discredits his testimony overall. He was fourteen when
he arrived in Australia, still a child, and his story
overall is consistent with his age and the things which,
in the absence of a psychological assessment and

physical examination, it is possible to at least speculate he has experienced.

I do not think his testimony as to his age is unconvincing and differ on this point from the hearing officer. He appears before me as a sixteen-year-old boy who knows when his birthday is and when the birthdays of all members of his family are, including his parents. Unlike many Iraqi families, his family seems to have made much of birthdays, and to have used western and Islamic calendars. He is able to consistently give the full names of his sister, cousins and parents when giving such trivial information. He has no problem saying how old he was when particular events took place in his country and answers this kind of question with an easy, frank and open manner. I am satisfied that he is who he says he is and that his stated age is correct.

Did he have effective protection in a safe third country? He states that, in hindsight, he believes his family to have been a major political target and that he would be very afraid to return 'as a man' to Syria. His evidence on the dangers of Syria to him personally is, however, hazy. He fled Syria when his friend told him that 'bad people' were after him. He knows nothing else. He was told by his father to never reveal his real name in Syria and so lived there under a false name, but he does not know why. He didn't even tell his friend his real name but stated his real name as soon as he arrived in Australia. He never went to

UNHCR offices in Syria, as he says he 'didn't think about being a refugee'. His friend in Syria, a 'businessman' of about fifty-five years of age, was his adviser and organised the trip with people smugglers, but the applicant insists that this was paid with his family's money. He does not know how much. He does not know how much money he had but 'almost all of it' was spent in the two years and on the people smugglers. It is worthy of note that he has more than $10 000 US dollars with him in Australia. He says this was put in his backpack by his friend and comes from his family's money.

Syria has been deemed to be safe for Iraqi returnees who have no particular interest to the Iraqi Government. Given that the applicant was very young when he was last in Syria, and lived there more or less safely for two years, on DFAT and consular advice he is very unlikely to represent a political target. I concur with the AID hearing officer in rejecting the claim that the applicant was in personal danger in Syria, although for the record I am convinced that he genuinely believes he was.

I find his fear of persecution in Syria, while genuine, to be unfounded. I find that Australia does not have protection obligations under the 1951 Convention in this case. I do have very grave concerns, however, about returning a traumatised unaccompanied

minor with no relatives to Syria and I recommend
Mr Dhurgham Assamarrai make an application for
a Special Humanitarian Visa Class A.

Dhurgham met a lawyer who was visiting Abu Nizar. He decided to go with Abu Nizar to his interview to keep him company, and because Abu Nizar told him that he should meet Mr Jean-Luc and learn a thing or two. He watched the lawyer with mild distrust. He had over the years absorbed a little of the guards' open hatred for lawyers and the bewilderment most people he knew felt at the inexplicable delays in every legal process. Jean-Luc Isakowski was a tousle-headed blond man with bright blue eyes and a serious face. He looked underslept. He asked Dhurgham, pen poised over Abu Nizar's fat file, where his case was at, and Dhurgham looked at him blankly for a moment.

'I have no real case,' he said. 'My memory is too unreliable.'

Mr Isakowski looked at him keenly for a moment and then sighed.

'How old are you?

'Nearly seventeen.'

'Family?'

Dhurgham hesitated. 'I don't know.'

Mr Isakowski sighed again and looked annoyed, or perhaps harassed. 'Do you have a lawyer? Have you ever spoken with a lawyer?'

'The AID lawyer helped me a lot.'

'When?'

'For my interview. Nearly two years, maybe.'

Mr Isakowski sighed for a third time and rummaged in his briefcase.

'I have seventy-three urgent cases. What is one more?' He pulled out a form, looked at Dhurgham with another glance of startling blue intensity and gave him a sweet smile. 'Fill this in,' he said gently. 'It will let me get all they have on your file and find out the story. I'll see what I can do to speed things up.'

A letter arrived for Dhurgham. He was sure there must be some mistake, but Abu Nizar told him that Australians had begun to write to some people, and they would have got his name and number from Mr Peter or Mr Jean-Luc. It was on plain paper. Abu Nizar held on tight to the paper and translated it for him, not remembering that Dhurgham could read English.

'*Welcome to Australia, Mr Assamarrai. I do hope you will be freed soon. I am sorry that our government has imprisoned you like this. I, and many other Australians feel for you, with all our hearts. These concentration camps are a great shame to our nation. I hope you have been able to contact your wife and children, and that they are all safe. If you would like to consider writing to me, my address is 68*

Sentinel Street, Bondi, NSW. If there is anything I can send you, please let me know. Yours faithfully, Joyce Collyer.'

There was a photo in the envelope of a middle-aged lady with a sad and imprecise face. She was seated on a bench surrounded by teddy bears with a tree he didn't recognise in the background and part of a low wire mesh fence in the foreground. She had a large Winnie Dubdoub on her lap. His heart twisted at that familiar yellow bear-face. The shadow of the person who took the photo, a man maybe, was splayed irregularly over the left-hand side teddy bears. Dhurgham kept the letter and photo in his things, stroking the paper and the words, imagining the friendliness of Joyce Collyer, but he didn't answer. He felt too tired.

Then, some weeks later, a bunch of flowers arrived for him from a Robin Tucker, whose address was 2A Semaphore Rd, Semaphore, SA. He sat on his bunk and fingered the strange blooms, feeling the pink and purple petals and yellow throats, rubbing them between his fingers, smelling the unfamiliar perfumes, unable to quite make them real but caught in them nonetheless. Then, on some impulse, he ate all but one of the flowers, savouring their odd vegetable taste. The last one, along with the succulent and poisonous-tasting green leaves, he gave to Mrs Azadeh. The bloom was big and pink with purple spots, with ochre yellow powder thick on its five delicate tongues. He watched the same dreamy unbelief float over Mrs Azadeh's features. He went to bed early, unbearably sad; and didn't write to Robin Tucker either.

But his heart warmed to the women in Australia. They seemed good to him, and he told himself that when he was free and could hold his head up, he would visit Semaphore SA and Bondi NSW and pay his respects to Joyce Collyer and Robin Tucker. He lost himself in a sweet dream in which he saw himself sitting upright and proud, just like his father, sipping coffee with guests, these two shadowy ladies, and both of them feeling pleased to have chosen this decent, upright Mr Dhurgham As-Samarra'i to write their welcomes to.

Hamdi al Yemeni and Mrs Zainuddin got the same letter and photo from Joyce Collyer. Dhurgham was bitterly disappointed in her at first, then told himself that only three people wasn't too bad, and at least he and Hamdi were male, and how could Joyce Collyer know anything about them anyway? But no one else got flowers from Robin Tucker and she became his favourite Australian friend. He imagined her with glasses and a kindly face, her children all grown up, a girl and a boy, now a doctor and a lawyer, with names like … Hilary and Bill. He imagined her in a garden, resplendent with exotic blooms coaxed out of the desert with incredible labours, with water running here and there to soak their roots, and he imagined her choosing the flowers he had eaten, cutting their sappy stalks and lovingly wrapping them in mauve paper. He would visit Semaphore first, then Bondi. Then he would pay a visit to Mr Jean-Luc in Adelaide and thank him warmly, pay him with Mr Hosni's money and offer to help him in all his fine humanitarian visa work.

> *FILE NOTE RRN230:*
> *Special Humanitarian Visa Class A application:*
> *Refused. The Minister has determined the applicant*
> *to have no special humanitarian priority. On findings*
> *of first hearing he is over eighteen years. See attached*
> *letter to Mr Jean-Luc Isakowski.*

Dhurgham and a hundred and fifty others received deportation notices. These warned him that he was liable for deportation as he had not lodged an appeal with the High Court within the statutory thirty-five days and in any case had no cause. Deportation would be carried out without warning.

In fact, Dhurgham and many others were a problem, as they could not be deported to Iraq. No country in the world was returning Iraqis. Another receiving country had to agree to have them. Syria had agreed quietly to receive some, for a fee of $10 000 per head, but with no guarantees; indeed, several deportees had vanished upon arrival in Damascus, not even seen by their waiting relatives.

Dhurgham presented a special problem, because Syria had refused him. In his AID file in Canberra was the following note:

'Deport him to Ghana, that's what Germany and
Sweden do. There are Arabs in Ghana, I believe. It's all
Africa.' Mr Trenoweth of AID had no patience with
these hold-ups. 'Do what you did with that
Liberian—we'll drop him in Côte D'Ivoire.'

'He's not African.' Chris Jensen had little time for
Mr Trenoweth, whom he regarded as an AID go-
between, although a powerful one at the Canberra end.
It was such a mess. Canberra, 3000 kilometres away,
made all the decisions without knowing anything
about the people in the centre. At times he wished he
could fly to Canberra, march into the Minister's office
and say, *They are not all the same, and what one will take*

144

with a smile, another will kill himself over. But Mr Jensen knew that if AID ordered a deportation to Ghana, he would have to authorise it. And he didn't feel good about the Liberian. The fellow didn't even speak French.

'Doesn't matter. Give the Ghanan officials enough money at the airport and they take him.'

'And then?'

'Look, he's a criminal here, a criminal there. He's scum. Better off in prison. Not our problem.'

'You're pretty sure of all that. I'm not so happy about this here, or anywhere else.'

'You don't get it. The world has changed. "Terrorism has changed the world." Some people, whether we like it or not, just don't belong any more. Once they start rushing about the globe, half-cocked, forum shopping, queue jumping, going about things the underhanded way, they step off the planet. And it's a cultural thing—they're all liars. Can't help it, never got anything in their lives except by lying.'

'Don't give me that. They might still buy that crap out there on the coast, or in Canberra, but at this end it's not so simple. Face facts. We don't want them, they don't fit, so we find ways to make people happy about getting rid of them. It's not pretty close up, and I'm the one here, not you. And this one, he's been here since well before all that.'

'You're are getting soft, Jensen. Let him go here and you'll find sooner or later he's just another potted terrorist. I told you, it's cultural. Anyway. Leave the deportation order with him. He might do something stupid and then we can put him in prison, or simply deport without qualms. It's not refoulement if he's a crim, is it now?'

Jensen sighed. He didn't correct Trenoweth. These Canberra wankers saw everything simplistically. He had a developing riot to contain and could do without the psychological games Canberra demanded he play with the inmates. And Trenoweth had a point. It was cultural. These people. He felt sorry for them, yes, but he was aware that he didn't like them. They were, generally, so devious. They lied. They were proud and brittle. They never thanked him, even when he bent over backwards for some of them. He sat staring at his overflowing desk after Trenoweth left. There were so many people to process, and here he was wasting time on a troublemaker teenager. And if, as Canberra said, Syria wouldn't have him, there was probably something wrong in the chain. Either a crim, yes, or a sensitive case; in other words, a refugee. The Minister would have to catch up with the paper-work and have the case heard again, or some lawyer would have to sniff it out for the injustices along the line. He was too tired, and sick of the many injustices that wriggled into the perfect system. He didn't like injustice.

It was cultural. They didn't fit. They were so unlike Australians. Praying and jumping up and down

146

about pork and fasting. It would be better for them and for Australia if they went home.

He swivelled around. On the wall behind the desk there was a smiling World Vision sponsor kid from Sudan and a photo of a shy-looking young man in subtly un-Australian clothes. Underneath each was a letter prominently displayed. He and Ann had decided that they had to sponsor a third-world child, and then they also sponsored the Muslim refugee from Bosnia into permanent settlement in Australia. It was a really good move. It reassured Rachel and Luke, set a good example. And leftie kids hassling them at school in Adelaide had been forced to shut up.

He turned back to his desk He had more staff on stress leave than he had ever had, and noises were being made that it was somehow his fault. Now he had to face the task of persuading his bosses to give him more teachers. Five hundred and seventy-nine children and three teachers was crazy.

Dhurgham dialled the number on the now grubby business card he had kept in his pocket since their meeting. He had liked feeling it now and then, as if it were a charm to ward off the evil eye. He fingered the plain blue print as the phone rang. Isakowski, Dempsey and Cranshaw, Solicitors. The line crackled and a woman answered. Dhurgham stuttered as he asked for Mr Jean-Luc, and then expelled his pent breath in relief when he heard that calm tired voice, tinny and far away. He blurted out his news.

'Deportation? No, I'll get an injunction. Don't worry about it. I'm still waiting to get Canberra's file and match up all AID records. Call me any time you need to, Thurgam.'

Mr Jean-Luc was the only person to ever try to use his real name.

> *The Australian*
> *Minister for Immigration, Ross Cowell said today that 1300 of the 1600 illegal aliens in processing centres today are not genuine refugees. 'Most are being held for deportation or appealing against deportation orders. They are exploiting pro bono lawyers to extend their stay in Australia and blocking up the courts.'*

The riot started with a seemingly small event and was, among AID guards, blamed directly on Dhurgham and Abu Rafik. After the event, though, neither was charged. Other ringleaders were identified and sent down to Adelaide in handcuffs.

Wildfires of crazy rumour sizzled and flared in the dry tinder of their boredom. Any chink for laughter or frenzy and Dhurgham would have taken it, just to feel his limbs move with speed and purpose, anything to unleash himself from the sleep that was dragging at him, anything to crack through the slow crust the desert seemed to settle on them. The guards were on edge. Dhurgham could see the spring in their step and feel their excitement. He understood without consciously articulating it: some of the guards wanted the chance to stand face to face as true enemies and to beat up their hated charges with all they had.

The air was electric with expectation, the sheds whispering with rumour. The flower-covered bus was there again, visible as a tiny, brightly coloured lozenge beyond the perimeter fence, its flowers blaring for attention across the red sand, trumpeting through the wire mesh, taking the eye out and away.

'The UN is here! The UN is here!' Maysam sang, scampering in and out among the adults. Some of the older boys took up the chant.

'Don't be silly—all over the world the UN drives Landcruisers, not buses covered in flowers,' Mr Hong muttered crossly next to Dhurgham.

'They are going to break us OUT! They are going to break us OUT!' screamed Maysam in his high voice, and Dhurgham started jumping up and down, waving to the faraway bus. The children began to rip off their shirts and throw them in the air, then to throw them high onto the sharp wire.

'Free-DOM! Free-DOM!' screamed Maysam, and that one got everyone going. It began as a low growl and rose to a roar, until everyone was screaming and shaking the fence. In the distance tiny banners unfurled, saying, *We Love You, Welcome*, and then, *Freedom for Refugees*.

The people behind the fence went wild.

The Freedom Bus was joined by the Hope Caravan on the second day, and more and more tiny colourful figures with placards gathered outside the far perimeter.

The Hope Caravan and Freedom Bus were visible day and night. At night campfires, torches and gas lamps made a faraway glittering city under a canopy of orange smoke out there in what had been the blank velvet dark of the desert. By the third day, the compound was taut with tension and grief. By midmorning the number of protesters with banners had swelled again. The children threaded their fingers in the wire of the perimeter fence and stared, dreamily. Men and women wept openly, both because there were people out there who cared about them, and because their imprisonment and hope-lessness suddenly became acute, stared them in the face, revealed. Mrs Azadeh sobbed on her knees in the red dust, throwing the sand in the air and then over her hair and face, wailing, 'We are not criminals! We are not criminals!' A protester with zoom lens filmed from the outer boundary until the AID guards approached Mrs Azadeh in riot gear, tranquillised her and dragged her away. The air was thick with grief and desperation and, for the younger kids, excitement and anticipation; so, all things considered, there probably would have been a riot no matter what.

• • •

Dhurgham was inside the recreation room with Abu Rafik. Abu Rafik forced Dhurgham to continue with his lessons, focusing on the Koran as he felt the boy slipping away. Dhurgham had as a boy learned key verses of the Koran off by heart, but not all of it, and, although he knew many of the verses and phrases that are part of daily life, in many cases he still didn't know the full Sura from which they came.

Abu Rafik demanded that he learn it, and recite it. 'Reciting the Koran is sacred. God's command "recite" brought the word of God into being. If you can recite the Koran, your soul can be free, can reach for belonging and being in Allah, in Mohammed, Peace Be Upon Him, and in all who have recited it before you. In reciting the Koran, you stand outside time, outside death.'

Dhurgham loved things like this, as Abu Rafik well knew, but in the week before Easter, time seemed to demand his presence and participation, and he chafed at the constraints of his lessons, chagrined that he might miss something exciting. He wanted to stand with the others and scream out his dreams at the Hope Caravan and the Freedom Bus.

Dhurgham's continuing recitation lessons were seen by the AID guards, even the sympathetic staff, as wrong and dangerous, a continuation of the banned school and an incantation directed against them and all they stood for, which some saw as AID, but others saw as democracy, the West, and freedom. More thoughtful staff, like Mr Peter, worried that Abu Rafik could not see the trouble the incomprehensible religious chant might bring, and saw the continuation of recitation lessons as unwise.

On the third day of the Hope Caravan protest, AID guards all donned riot gear as a precaution in the rising tension, and this seemed to unleash something in both the guards and the inmates. Mr James, who was an older man, generally kindly, and should have known better, marched up to Abu Rafik and Dhurgham in the re-creation room. Dhurgham was dressed in a clean white qamis, quietly reciting the Surat al Rahman from the book, with Abu Rafik listening. Mr James snatched the Koran from his hands and threw it to the floor. He was so annoyed that he didn't notice all the men rise in the recreation room around him. They might have been seated without the orderly appearance of the former school, but they were all listening to Dhurgham and Abu Rafik.

'Stop that mumbo jumbo. Learn English, and get your head and arse out of the dark ages. It fries your brains and it's driving me crazy. Can't you see all the evil in the world is coming from this?'

Abu Rafik rose, looked Mr James in the eye angrily, then stiffly got down on his knees to retrieve the book.

James Williams was never officially reported for what followed. He kicked the holy book from the old man's fingers and brought his baton down onto the back of Abu Rafik's neck and head. The room went wild. Dhurgham leapt upon Mr James, twining his arms around the older man's neck as Abu Rafik struggled to his feet and tried to pull Dhurgham off. It was as if someone had finally put a match to a huge bonfire. Every man in the room shouted at once, then one began raising a chair up and smashing it down on computers, at windows and against the walls. Within seconds everyone was armed with chairs, keyboards, broomsticks and was kicking and battering. They turned on the building, on the things around them, rather than on James Williams or the two other guards, one of whom backed out of the room and ran. Someone somehow set fire to the drawings stacked in a corner, and then thirty guards burst in with shields and batons. The centre erupted almost simultaneously from end to end, and the idea of fire seemed to have been shared by telepathy.

Dhurgham went mad with the release the riot brought. He was ripped off Mr James' back to struggle in delight and fury against the guards, screaming abuse. In the chaos he managed to wriggle his way outside, still screaming. He forgot what happened with the Koran and Abu Rafik completely, so wonderful was the explosion all around him. He was as euphoric as if the bus and caravan had driven in, busted down the fence and flown away with them into the sky. He sprinted up and down the compound screeching with adolescent happiness at the burning buildings and the advancing troops of his enemies, his arms outstretched.

He didn't even see the water cannon until it knocked him flat.

FILE NOTE RRN230:
A ringleader in the Easter riots. Strongly influenced by POZ114, who is his self-appointed religious teacher. Confined for three days. To be monitored. No charges at this time.

The week after the riots and fires, a pall hung over the centre, smelling of smoke and ash and failure. The dongas were in silent lock-down and the solitary confinement cells in Paradise were full. Dhurgham was released from confinement to his donga almost immediately once lock-down ended, but he couldn't go and see Abu Rafik, who stayed two weeks in confinement as a ringleader. A few men were sent away to prison in Alice Springs to await trial as the ringleaders proper, even though two of them hadn't done more than shout. For some reason Abu Rafik wasn't chosen. The day he was released, Dhurgham, hearing the news from Mr Peter, made his way immediately to Ammu's donga.

He knocked but there was no answer. However, there were the tiny noises that a thin house makes with someone in it, so Dhurgham pushed in.

Ammu was hanging from the fan, dangling between the bunks, slowly turning, face away. Dhurgham felt his heart die and for a moment couldn't move. Ammu's hands and legs moved in pain and the fan slowly turned him face to face with Dhurgham. His eyes stood out in his bruised-looking skull, and his lips moved as his fingers flicked outward urgently. Dhurgham saw the cold soundless lip-mouthed words fall like stones to the floor even as he found his own limbs again and surged forward as if in a dream to grab Ammu's legs, brace himself against the bunk beds and lift. When he laid Ammu on the bed he could not look at him.

Get out. Get out. Leave me. You ... are ... not ... my son.

Later, Dhurgham sank onto his bunk, watching his own fan go round and round. His body ached and buzzed. His neck and shoulders were so tight he couldn't turn his head properly. Ammu's face turned again and again towards him, cracked white lips moving. He felt as though he had been slashed open. He could barely breathe. Then suddenly his memory cleared for a split second and he saw his father, kneeling in the starlight beside the black hump of a backpack, praying. His uncle stood, body restless, murmuring to his huddled family. Nura and his mother were embracing the women, the children, kissing them, and his uncle was moving away in the darkness. They had all already kissed him. He could still smell their perfumes and face cream pressed into his skin. Their backs were to him, then they were gone. His father rose, shouldered the pack and stared upwards. Dhurgham latched onto that face, those shining eyes, the black moustache, the glint of white teeth. This was it. He would see it all, and know. His heart raced. He would finally see the blood, the terrible wounds, the writhing, the cracked lips, the last words that his memory had shut away from him. He would finally know if it was capture or murder, and what his mother and father and sister gave him in their last glances. He tried to still his heart in case it dislodged this, shook it loose and he lost it again in the depths. His father turned and spoke, softly. 'My darling, my life, this is it. Princess, come to me.' And for once Nura let herself be hugged, so Dhurgham rushed up to them both, his father and sister, and wrapped his arms around their ribs. He could smell them both, smell Nura's hair and his father's sweat. He could hear his mother wheezing behind them.

'Freedom and safety, then,' his father said.

'Shhhh,' his mother gasped, breathing noisily.

They all held hands and stepped out into the low marshlands. His hand was in Nura's on one side and his father's on the other. Then he lost them utterly as if they stepped out into the ocean and sank out of sight.

Abu Rafik's attempt to kill himself shattered some spell. Something in Dhurgham was to that point still so sunny that he didn't often question his own importance, especially to those who cared for him. Without ever making the thought conscious, he had felt that he gave Abu Rafik as much life as he got from him, and this was true. But Dhurgham had seen this as a young child would. And Abu Rafik's words shamed him. Of course he was not Ammu's son! Did Ammu think he was a baby? Did Ammu try to kill himself to get away from Dhurgham?

Dhurgham writhed. He *had* assumed that he was the centre of Abu Rafik's universe, and the thought that Abu Rafik could desire freedom more was very terrible to him. It was far worse than Marwa.

Dhurgham slipped into a depression that began with pique but from there unravelled him.

Dhurgham stopped attending any classes. Ammu was gone, sent to a psychiatric hospital in Adelaide, and Dhurgham's heart flooded with desolation and abandonment. Why was he alone? It was not a question that could be answered with the loss of his parents, the suicide attempt of Ammu, the utter absence of Nura, the parting with Mr Hosni, with all the real or imagined reasons for these. It could not be answered by his memory abandoning him. Why was he alone? His fellow inmates were not. They yearned for family who longed in return for a word, or sight of them. They had family, children to scream at, to cuff, and then weep with. They had cousins, brothers, husbands, living in

Australian cities, waiting every day for their release. He had had Ammu, but when he asked a guard if he could phone Ammu in hospital, the guard said, 'Fuck off, poofta.'

Dhurgham was alone. The crust stiffened over him, stilling his heart, and he found that he could not drag himself out of his bunk to queue for breakfast, and didn't care if he missed the queue for lunch. The centre was changing rapidly, but he found he was unable to take any pleasure in the novelty of Nintendo and Foxtel, newly painted murals, fake lawn or anything else. He had Mr Jean-Luc's card in his things. He had the memory of a sweet smile, and the invitation to call the phone number any time if he was worried, but he couldn't bring himself to ask a guard for phone time, even though there were now far more phones and no longer the restrictions and discomforts of being 'accompanied' during the call. Mr Peter came to drag him to school, with gentle words and cajolements, with promises that he could have more time in the art room, that he could stay when the little children had their class, just to do something to keep his mind alive. Dhurgham came quietly, a few times, more out of love and respect for Mr Peter than anything else, and he did find himself distracted, even happy at school, but the next morning he found again that he couldn't move. Mr Peter bought him a sketch pad and some pencils to use in his room, something that was sternly for-bidden, and Dhurgham sometimes drew, trying not to remember the beautiful pictures he had drawn for Mr Hosni, or the paintings Mr Hosni had done, saying Dhurgham was the inspiration.

He began cartoons and, slowly, these took over.

Chris Jensen told Peter that Dhurgham was eighteen or older and not to bother with school if he didn't turn up. Only kids under twelve were really supposed to get lessons.

Mr Peter forced him to see a doctor and he was prescribed tablets for depression and tablets to make him sleep. He said out loud to himself later, on his bunk: 'Give me freedom, or torment me, but don't torment me and then give medicine to treat the symptoms.' Ammu had said that. Those very words. If only he had remembered and said them to the doctor!

'Tom.'

Dhurgham looked up from his bed. He was alone in the donga and, in the glaring light of the open door, he couldn't make out who was there, only that it was a guard. He sat up. Officer Anders stepped in awkwardly, glanced behind him and shut the door, taking his hat off. Dhurgham stiffened.

'RRN 230, to you, sir,' he said quietly.

Officer Anders sat down on one of the bunks, looking at his dusty shoes. Then he looked up. 'I'm sorry, Tom, about what happened with—' He looked down. He had nice ears, red now, Dhurgham thought. But nice. Shapely around his young, close-cropped head. With his blond dome bowed low, he looked as though he might be praying.

Officer Anders looked up again, and met Dhurgham's gaze. 'I am leaving today. I feel bad, because —Look, mate, I'm sorry for calling you a refusee.'

Dhurgham held his gaze, feeling out this changed relationship, almost savouring it for the long-ago person he could have been in it, not sure quite what to say. The walls ticked in the heat around them. He smiled without warmth at Officer Anders' blushing young face.

'Fuck you,' he said.

Chris Jensen was tired, but he couldn't sleep. Rachel's words played over and over in his mind.

'Dad, you would know him better than me—he was in your processing centre for two years.'

He wished he hadn't asked her what Aziz was like. He had been thrown.

Rachel had rushed in from school. 'Dad, you know those boys from the news, Aziz Abdul Something and Mohammad Basri? They're going to our school! Aziz is in my class!'

He had said then that he didn't know the boy—
there were so many. He knew that Rachel knew that
he lied.

He had felt a wave of strange fear. It was too close
to home. What if the boy knew that Rachel was his
daughter? *Of course* the boy knew that Rachel was his
daughter—everyone in the school knew that Rachel
was his daughter. He had had a hard job, a terrible job,
running the centre, and it wasn't personal. But you
never knew what they said to each other—and what
if one of them took it personally?

He did remember Aziz. He remembered himself
saying to a defiant dark face, in a moment of stress and
anger, 'I'm personally going to make sure you NEVER
get a visa.'

He couldn't remember what Aziz had done to
provoke it.

Then, suddenly, as he sat on the toilet at 1 am, the
memory flooded him with the smell of shit.

Aziz had smeared the solitary room with his own
excrement. He had written Arabic words all over the
walls in a stinking rage. The prisoners Chris called in to
clean it up had clucked their tongues in disapproval,
but smirked quietly to themselves, and Chris had just
lost it.

What if, in the end, they all got out? Dhurgham
Samurai, Aziz's best friend? Mahmoud al Haqqi?

In the dead of night Chris Jensen finally thought
it—he had only done his job, and he had done it well,

but he didn't want most of these long-term desperadoes out and around his family. It was a revenge culture after all. Even the quiet, meek ones, the ones who had been good, the ones he'd helped. You could never really know what they were thinking. Their meekness was no more than a strategy. At 2 am he was regretting helping any of them.

Then he thought of Irshad. He had adored that bright, warm-hearted little boy, with his archaic, little-old-man manners. So had Ann. So had the guards. They had all done everything they could for Irshad. Ann even helped get the Minister to intervene and release him.

He couldn't sleep.

The question rang on and on into the predawn: did it all really depend on whether you were loved, lovable?

Chris Jensen left suddenly. He was replaced by Donald Riordan. Overnight new policies regulated everything, from the order in the queue for lunch to the interactions between all staff and inmates. All inmates suddenly stopped receiving their usual volume of mail and phone calls.

Some of the older men complained and Mr Donald himself came to give them a lecture in the prayer donga.

'You were probably much like us once, but centuries of Islam have cultivated the worst in you.

You have all the human traits we have, and vice versa. But where your first inclination would be violence, ours would be forbearance; where yours would be revenge, ours forgiveness. Do you see what I am getting at? You are primitives. You don't value your kids enough. You kill women when you feel dishonoured by them. And you people have no proper control of sexuality, and are driven to imprison women because of it. All your crime and terrorism comes from that. Like little kids. It's a mess. You see what I mean? We are both basically the same, you and I. But your culture has fucked you up.'

Angry murmurs spread through the men and women in front of him.

It was a grim time in the centre, even though the centre itself had never looked better. The population was down. The letters and flowers and presents from the Australians somewhere beyond the horizon no longer came, except for those who had established friendships across the vast stretch of desert, and even these dried to a trickle. All certainties withered. Guards who had been friendly became unapproachable. Staff who had been gentle became brittle, exhausted and disappeared with the same suddenness and at almost the same rate as the inmates. The long-term inhabitants seemed unable to go near anything sharp without slashing themselves, or near anything chemical without drinking it. It was in the air, in the culture of the centre. If you could, you did. It was a relief. Someone

163

discovered that you could cut yourself in the corner capping of the jaunty new dongas, and soon everyone was doing it and the dongas had to be redesigned. Some of them had begged, by now, to be deported to face their chances in Iran, Iraq or Afghanistan, and the general despair increased when even these men and women stayed.

Mr Donald had almost half the population on high-alert surveillance, or 'suicide watch', and thirty percent of his staff on stress leave.

Abu Nizar was a quiet man. He never complained. He had been almost completely silent since Mrs Azadeh got her visa and settled in some hypothetical place called Albany, made all the more unreal by her descriptions in her first letter to him. Dhurgham loved him. Abu Nizar was the horologist, after all. The only man who understood in intricate detail the mystery of what they were enduring. When he told Dhurgham three times that his back hurt and there was blood in his urine, Dhurgham forced him to go to a nurse.

Abu Nizar nearly left the queue when he saw Miss Cora was on duty, but Dhurgham cajoled and pleaded, calling him Uncle.

No one liked to see Miss Cora.

Miss Cora looked at Abu Nizar coldly and threw three Panadol tablets at his feet. Abu Nizar didn't bend to pick them up.

'Are we animals, that you treat us like this?' Abu Nizar seemed to be choking. He never spoke so loudly.

Dhurgham had never heard Abu Nizar raise his voice. He stared, worried, at the older man's drawn face.

'You are lower than animals,' Miss Cora said and turned her back to them.

Dhurgham said nothing and left quietly with Abu Nizar.

Abu Nizar climbed onto the roof that afternoon. He shouted over and over, 'I want my watch! Where is my father's gold watch!' and tapped his wrist repeatedly. Then he slashed himself open across the belly with some glass he had been hiding before the guards swarmed up and beat him down with batons. Abu Nizar disappeared, transported in the night to a hospital in Adelaide. When he returned two weeks later, he was put in isolation and for some reason never released in all the remaining time Dhurgham was there. Dhurgham asked about him now and then and was told he was still there, fine, but could not be visited. He took it calmly, without question, without frowning.

Dhurgham was put on the high-alert surveillance list, and he found that with the tablets came constant intrusions to check that he had not harmed himself, and more frequent room searches. He started to imagine shocking them by harming himself. It gave him a lot of pleasure. AID didn't care for him! No, not at all. It would just look bad if someone died and they couldn't cover it up. He wished he could die just to show them up and then come back and gloat.

He had come to like his number. He felt powerful every time he signed a cartoon RRN 230. He referred to himself ironically, playing the fool, the mad prisoner who has forgotten his real name. But this also made him feel armoured and that was a good thing, here in this room.

He drew the wriggly butterfly line on the white page that made his Australia. Its skin. Its spread. The first time he'd traced it out from an atlas in the recreation room it had been as seemingly random as a water stain dried into the page. Now it was absolute. Fixed. More firm than the shocking, cold stars in the sky above Mawirrigun. He could do it now with his eyes shut. His face was dreamy. This line was mantric, a chant filled with the need to repeat and repeat.

He drew a stylised flame off-centre, the heart. It might be a campfire, warming him. But this was Mawirrigun. This was the X marking the spot where he, RRN 230, sat. This flame was both his prison and himself. Flame, rose, dagger, heart (cleft)—this symbol, in this spot, whatever he drew, also required no thought. Mawirrigun was forever.

Then he divided Australia from top to bottom with a careful but wavering line. The Highway. The one road in the red desert to the north of Mawirrigun, to the south of Mawirrigun. The one road to and from forever. He felt utterly calm as his blood stilled into the drawing.

Today he drew the Highway as a zipper, opening down—opening that blank unknown country, to what? In the start of that V was nothingness. He drew slanting rainfall and under it a multifoliate rose, rising out of the zipper. Himself.

In that V, in the opening up of the red highway, in the splitting of the desert by rain and in the desert flowers, there he would find himself. One day. Outside forever and back into the rush of a sunset and the wind roaring past an open window and the sound of a diesel engine, steady and dependable, rushing away and unzipping the world. Behind him flowers. The sempiternal foliage of the mosque mosaic formed unasked from his pen.

Another day he began the same cartoon, trying to perfect it, but when he drew the open zipper and tried on inspiration to draw the AID Minister Cowell peeping out, Mr Hosni's grinning face flooded from his pen onto the page.

Dhurgham went on hunger strike. The heat shimmered around him and inside him. The weaker he got, the more he felt that he was glowing with the heat. Here, here was the power and the glory he had lost all this while! Here in his empty belly and his legs and arms that could no longer carry him! He thought of the curling leaves and glinting mosaics. He found he could remember with clarity every curl, every frond, every ancient façade and stair, and he lost himself in ageless grandeur. He thought of the ocean rising and falling under the holy light of the sun and he dived singing into its coolness and drowned. He was a saint and a devil, a dagger in the sides of the guards. He reached into his memory for the stillness and not the anxiety, for the beauty and not the stink. Without moving his head from his bed he could feel their discomfort and his resolve strengthened. He had been thus on the boat, yes. He was strong. Stronger than these guards and these soft voices, and stronger than these flimsy walls, these metal barricades! He soared in a waking dream, ecstatic in his burning bed, joyous, vicious, exultant.

What Peter saw when he went to visit Dhurgham with Don Riordan's message was different from what he had expected. He saw a bone-thin teenage boy lying flat on a bed, huge black eyes burning but otherwise motionless. Dhurgham pulled dry lips back over sticky yellow teeth in a grimace and whispered, 'I am stronger than all of you.' Peter didn't see the joy. He only saw a boy with fetid breath who should have been using his muscles and mind, wasting away in a feverish madness.

'Tom,' he said quietly, 'I have been told to tell you that you are to be forcibly fed and given water unless you stop this nonsense now.'

Dhurgham's laugh was like a wind in sedge. 'I am stronger,' he whispered again.

Dhurgham was cuffed to the bed by one hand and both feet. Miss Cora held his head to stop him threshing. A new guard he hadn't seen before straddled his stomach. Mr Theo held his arm and the nurse inserted a cannula and attached it to a drip. Dhurgham fell asleep almost instantly and didn't wake for three days.

Without warning, Dhurgham was moved out of Mawirrigun to Kanugo Kagil 3000 kilometres to the east. Mr Donald called him into his office, told him that this was in preparation for him to be deported, forcibly if he refused to go, and then the guards put him on the darkened bus without letting him return to his room and get his shoes. It all happened in a split second, then there was the numbing bus journey—a sequence of strange, bleak service stations and an armed guard at his toilet door, and then for days he felt himself sitting like a ghost in his new room, taking his time to catch up with his body.

Two hours after he left, Jean-Luc Isakowski arrived for the appointment he had confirmed with AID staff a week before. He was met with blank looks and then assurances that his client had been transferred, that his client had expressly stated that he didn't want to see Mr Isakowski because he was a Jew, and that his client was now in Kanugo Kagil. Mr Isakowski rang Kanugo Kagil. RRN 230 was not there either but was expected. He sighed and asked resignedly to see his other clients. He packed up his doubts at the end of the day and got in his outdated car and drove the fifteen hours back to Adelaide to try to find out what had really happened.

Once Dhurgham caught up with himself and had time to think it over and feel Mawirrigun sink into the past and dreams, the move to Sydney set a small clock ticking. It broke his Australia open and gave it form, colour, dimension. The momentum of the move from desert to city could not be stilled. In Kanugo Kagil he was wound up, waiting, he wasn't sure what for, but he knew that he couldn't stay, not long. The energy charging him day and night had to carry him out and away. Kanugo Kagil looked like a prison but it wasn't, not entirely. It was too sloppy, much sloppier than Mawirrigun. The worst guards and security officers could indulge in behaviour far less controlled than in a prison; the best could be far gentler and more indulgent. The place had so much regulation that was invented to annoy that its regulations for smooth management and policies of basic procedure were eroded, highly variable. Dhurgham noted all this with pleasure.

Kanugo Kagil had no electrified outer perimeter fence. It had the jagged wire scroll over the top, but the single fence itself seemed to him amazingly permeable. At one point he could stand, fingers locked through that single scaly skin, and look straight out into a cracked asphalt lane leading past miscellaneous brick walls and an overhang of jasmine, past an old, upturned green rubbish bin to a street lamp. He could see the exotic peaks of red and orange tiled roofs. In the distance he could hear a clock chime, on the half-hour, on the hour. He could feel himself to be a crooked finger's breadth from a return to life. He could hear its hum and bustle, its measured paces, its rituals. The scurry in the morning, horns blaring, to work and to school. The scurry home, the settled quiet. Its monitors: the clock and the intermittent sirens. His fingers could push through into air in which the police tracked down the bad people and the ambulances rescued the hurt people; and fires were put out without anyone being beaten up. And the clock.

Curiously, he knew none of the people in his compound. Some he mistook at first for visitors, as less than half were Arab, Iranian or Afghan. He had expected to find Rafik and others who had been transported, but they were long gone. Some knew of them and could tell him that they were released or deported, or hospitalised, but none of this seemed real. Dhurgham had no hope of release. But he had growing hope of freedom. His fear kept him awake and alert, and his spirits remained high.

● ● ●

He didn't plan his escape. He kept himself to himself, quiet, uncommunicative. He was still on high surveillance but he paid no attention to the intrusions. He prayed. No one knew him here, so he rebuilt himself as a quiet, devout, good man: a horologist. Within two weeks he was rewarded and taken off the list. He began to avoid taking his drugs when he could. He needed to be alert, to miss nothing. He waited and watched for his escape to be made manifest to him. He put all his trust in God.

When the single fence parted in front of him, he was unsurprised. He barely heard the grunts and gasps of the two men. He didn't feel their fear or urgency. He heard the clang of the miraculous two-handled cutters as they fell slowly to ground, and he flowed like water through the breach, singing.

Eleven men struggled through after him, only six part of any plan, before the hole was plugged in a shriek of sirens and hoarse shouting. But Dhurgham was with God. He was long gone, running far and fast in the windswept streets, moving, inspired, into a maze of alleys; leaping to hide, inspired, in an enclosed private garden. He sang quietly as he sat on a wooden garden bench under a sweet-smelling tree with a smooth white trunk.

A song then welled up in him. It seemed to come from somewhere beneath his belly, deep from the well of his childhood. It was the radio play theme song of the great knight and warrior Sayf bin Dhi Yazan, who arose from the East, blessed with a green spot on his cheek, fated to revenge his father's murder, to unite the warring clans in an empire and to love his beloved. He set the land aflame in victory, glory and ultimately tragedy. It was silly. He smiled to himself. He *did* feel sort of heroic. He *had* stood up, seized back his self and walked away, as he had once thought they all had to.

He was encircled by flowers. It wasn't Joyce Collyer's garden, he could tell. He was probably nowhere near Bondi. He wasn't even sure Bondi existed. He stroked the Australians' white, golden-eyed cat, his hands quivering in delight, his heart filled with love. It had been so long since he had touched a creature! He trusted the rhythm of the city that he would be safe until about six-thirty, and then, when he heard the chime, nearer now, he stopped humming and hid in a dusty woodshed filled with aromatic resinous logs until God brought down the curtain of night and flooded the place with slanting rain. His heart beat like a furnace bellows; God's blessed cat purred against his chest and he stayed warm.

He had left Mr Hosni's money and presents behind. He had left everything that had anything to do with Mr Hosni. It felt good.

III

hurgham sat across from Mr Johns, the immigration official sent to interview him. His first glimpses of New Zealand had been of an impossible green, and his heart had jumped. Mountains, red flowering trees, a glittering white-washed city. So green. Unlike Australia. Utterly unlike. But he could not afford to hope. Just to express himself clearly. The interview rooms were demountables on the wharf. They had no windows and had cream-coloured impermanent-looking walls. He was in an evanescent non-place that he recognised. This was not yet New Zealand. He was not yet there. Not yet. He stared at the dictaphone in the middle of the table.

'Now, Mr … Samurai, tell me again what you told Ms Matehaere,' Mr Johns said, leaning forward.

Dhurgham was silent for a moment, the much-practised phrase suddenly eluding him. He blushed.

Then it came, in his most perfect English. He spoke with the rhythm of an incantation, the same he would use in Arabic for seeking refuge from Satan.

'I seek protection under the 1951 Convention and Protoc-c-col. I am a refugee.'

Mr Johns noticed the blush. The boy was very young. Maybe eighteen at the most, although with these kids you couldn't tell. Wiry and ancient at twelve. A dark, closed, secretive face. An ugly, almost obsequious manner.

'What is your nationality?'

'I am from al Iraq.'

Yes, Mr Johns thought. *Probably malnutrition, military exercises, probably a hard life.*

'Where did you learn English?'

'In Australia.'

Mr Johns sat up, bewildered, and eyed the boy. Dhurgham said quickly, stumbling, 'I am refugee from Australia. Australia treat me very bad. No human rights.' He paused. 'I have fear of persecution in Iraq and in Australia. I am double refugee.'

Mr Johns laughed out loud and Dhurgham blushed again.

'An escaped criminal from Australia, more like,' he said, still smiling. Dhurgham didn't smile or respond. Didn't protest. His skinny hand on the table began to shake.

Mr Johns made a mental note of it. What to do? The Arab had said the right things, had obviously studied the right things to say. Hell, he probably *was* a refugee from Iraq. Everyone who left, just about, would be, from the scum on the streets to the, well, merchants, thieves, belly-dancers or whatever. But Australia. You had to laugh.

'You are the first,' he said slowly, 'to *ever* ask to be protected from Australia!' Dhurgham in front of him smiled a strange inward smile, and Mr Johns saw for a moment the face of a very beautiful young boy shine through the shifting, hunched cunning. Dhurgham had begun to shake all over, then began to speak in a rush, raising his dark eyes for the first time to Mr Johns' face.

He leant forward over the dictaphone and said loudly, 'Four years in p-p-p-prison with only one T-shirt. I am from a good family, with good clothes. They treat me like a criminal. They say I am liar, use filthy words. They tie me.' He held out his wrists in an eloquent gesture, the base of the palms pressed together, and Mr Johns noticed scabby scars on both wrists.

'Tie me. Tie me!' There was no reaction that Dhurgham could see and he struggled to find more words. 'No trial! No hope! Prison for the life! In Australia no human rights!'

The man in front of him looked blank. Not smiling anymore. Dhurgham felt like crying and then suddenly he was. Even though he could see that this made Mr Johns dislike rather than pity him, he couldn't stop. He was tired. He had escaped and in this green green land he could tell that it was going to be no different. The old feeling of self-disgust rose up in a wave and washed over him. Those who left the camps in just a few months, those were the truly good people, no blemish on them. Chosen people. Even al Haj was among the chosen people. All his bravado and false confidence washed away and he knew that he could not speak another word of English.

Mr Johns watched the thin shoulders bowed in front of him, the scruffy black hair. It could not have been an easy trip. Yachts are not comfortable, even the big ones, and staying undetected in a forward hatch under folded sails until the last day would have been extremely difficult. He was still more than a bit suspicious of the skipper. The fact that the man was a Queen's Counsel made it hard to accuse him, though. He felt dizzy. It was ludicrous really. Australia had good reasons for the imprisonment of illegal immigrants, convention claimants or otherwise. Very good reasons, what with September Eleven and all. This boy had obviously been rejected as a refugee and had lived in limbo. No western country, no signatory to the Convention, would forcibly deport someone to certain persecution, so Mr Samurai would have been a bit stuck. But as soon as Mr Johns thought this, he felt dizzy again. It was ludicrous. He found himself staring at the scabs circling the boy's extended wrists. Four years. And Mr Johns knew that Australia excluded refugees from invoking her protection obligations on technicalities a lot of the time. Safe third country clauses, seven-day rule and all that.

'I'll refer you to have your case for refugee status considered,' he heard himself saying. He closed the interview, pressing the stop button on the dictaphone. He got up, almost throwing his chair down behind him, and left the room without looking back, his head spinning. He could see the headlines. He could suddenly see himself losing his job, Janine quiet and bitter, furious and drawn with worry. The mortgage and Carrie's education.

But for one second he had seen Dhurgham as a boy arriving by boat in Australia. Just an ordinary boy, maybe thirteen or fourteen. Maybe if they were lucky, he was a criminal and could be returned to serve his term. But Mr Johns knew that Dhurgham was right in one thing at least. He had never been tried or convicted. That was not what Australia, or New Zealand for that matter, spent tax payers' money on in handling convention claimants. Dhurgham was a boy imprisoned without trial indefinitely in Australia and would be immediately imprisoned if he were deported back there. He also knew that by escaping, Dhurgham had now broken Australian law and would probably go straight to an ordinary prison, not even a processing centre. All the words running through his head began to turn and present ugly faces. Term of his natural life. No trial. An imprisoned minor. Refugee. A boy who was swallowed and his future gone until, probably with some bravery, he escaped and fled to New Zealand. If you looked at it from the point of view that Dhurgham was a boy who knew only what he had seen and experienced, and was not a unit in a growing batch of failed convention claimants who were from a country to which they could not be returned, then it was not a comfortable sight. For a moment Mr Johns had seen black, intense eyes filled with the awful vulnerability of too much confusion and too little hope. Eyes you shouldn't see on a kid. He wished Dhurgham had stayed shifty, not looked up. Because suddenly even shifty could be explained on a boy imprisoned for years in a strange, hostile country with no reason that he could understand. Dhurgham's body had begged and grovelled, but his eyes had been too frank with something he had not said in words. Mr Johns had a headache. Mr Johns did not like his vision one bit.

He checked into his office and said he was going home early.

'What?' Janine Johns was laughing. 'Bloody cheek! What did you do!'

'I think he is a refugee, on the face of it. Probably on both counts.'

Janine put her hand over her mouth, her eyes popping out in glee at him. She was obviously imagining the political furore, the papers. The savage happiness a New Zealander can feel when she annoys the Australian nation. But even Janine's delight could not cheer him up. He had imagined all the same things with no pleasure at all.

'You signed him in for a *hearing*? He's an escapee! Why didn't you just deport him!' Mr Harwood was very annoyed. 'Of all the bleeding hearts!'

But Mr Johns was both more unhappy and more certain of what he had done having slept on it. He stood silent as his boss paced back and forth.

'I don't like it one bit,' he said, finally, 'but indefinite impris—'

'Processing.'

'—whatever, with no trial—'

'He's not a citizen.'

'He's not a criminal.'

'Well you've fucked up good and proper. What are we going to do? If the media—' Mr Harwood's voice trailed off.

The media loved stirring Australia like an ants' nest. They also both knew that since the Tampa affair, New Zealand was in Australia's good books, and that the golden sun of the wheat and beef kingdom had been shining their way.

'It's *Australia*, for God's sake!'

'Probably what Turkey says about—' Mr Johns struggled to find a country adjoining Turkey. 'Jordan.'

There was a silence.

'I'll get Josie to do the hearing,' Mr Harwood said thoughtfully. 'He speaks English, you said, so no interpreter necessary. Josie's tough. She'll catch him lying, and problem solved.'

'He'll still be a refugee,' Mr Johns muttered but Mr Harwood wasn't listening. He already had the phone to his ear.

'Josie's on leave? Since when? Bloody hell—'

Dhurgham slept his first night in New Zealand in a cell of Mount Crawford. This time he was not surprised that he was in a prison. The bed was clean, the room was warm and he was utterly exhausted. He curled up like a small, sick animal and drifted away on his own thoughts as soon as they locked the door.

It had been a long, cold day. He had had to leave behind the warm woollies he had worn on the yacht. He was floating, not imagining any next step. The drive from the demountable on the pier to the prison had been in a heated car. As his body slowly warmed he had looked out over the bay and marina with a feeling of intense loneliness. Which mast was the *Morning Star*? Had they sailed already, or were they eating and drinking, now, talking lovingly about him? A tear slipped down his cheek and he brushed it away roughly. Wellington at dusk was beautiful. Windows here and there up the mountain glittered with the reflection of the orange sea. The prison overlooked the strait from a small green mountain just a few minutes, it seemed, out of the city.

On that sea, just seven hours ago, he thought, I was free.

He was a world away from the yacht. It might have been a dream but for the rise and fall his body still played over and over like a favourite song.

Skipper Joe's first words. *Fuck me mother, what the blazing bejesus are you doing here?*

Dhurgham smiled. Maybe he should have gone with them to South America.

EnZed will take care of you. Women in power, in Enzed.

Dhurgham's imaginary New Zealand had at that moment become a motherland.

What's your name?

Dhurgham, sir. Dhurgham As-Samarra'i.

Fuck me. Make it Tom. Call me Skipper or Joe. Now, what's the story?

Dhurgham stared up at kindly New Zealand's prison ceiling. He smiled.

Hey youse fuckers! Get down here! We've got a refugee. It's fucken raining boat people.

He had had a strange feeling on that boat that the whole time in Australia was a dream, and that he had never left the open ocean, never left the fishing boat. God had taken the boat of boys and made it sail on into happiness, transformed from fear to calm, from innocence to experience, from boys to old men, sailing on forever.

The *Morning Star* didn't resemble the fishing boat at all. Nor did it resemble the boat he had dreamed of in Indonesia. It was a small ketch, painted white on the hull and coach-housing. It was all polished timber and brass inside the cabin, which was set out like a tiny imaginary house. Green seats, a table with a lip to stop things from sliding off, a toy wooden parrot swinging over the table, brass-ringed navigation instruments, brass lanterns, ingeniously designed stowage and book-shelves lining the berth. It berthed four, but there was always someone on watch, so they never felt the squeeze of being five. Dhurgham used every berth in turn. The timbers were gold and deep red, lovingly done. The galley was quaint and stylish, and easy to use. It was stocked to the brim with food and drink. It even had a toilet and shower, called, for no reason Dhurgham could guess, a head. The whole dreamy little house was permanently tilted, permanently moving, giving it a strange self-sufficiency all its own. *This is normal*, it said, *you outlandish dill, you foolish stranger.* To Dhurgham it was like the insides of a sea creature, and they were cheery men swallowed forever by a whale. There was no happier way to be.

It was, he thought happily, his *Mayflower*. His *Endeavour*. He was, after all, a great traveller now, like Ibn Battuta.

Joe, Gino, Stan and Jim were grey, hairy irreverent men who made obscure jokes and whose professions were at first impossible to guess. *We're fucken professors, barristers and drug dealers. Now people smugglers*, Joe said, winking at him. *We're the elitist bleedin' hearts, at y' service.* Four joking men who sailed with delight and loved the sea. Dhurgham felt his nightmares wash away with waves. Each terrible memory of his other journey was taken individually, washed clean and handed back to him transformed and beautiful. He was fed well and too often. He was safe. The great swell lifted and dropped him without breaking the calm. The dolphins were to be merely admired. He sat on deck in the sun with them, tipsy on champagne and other alcohols they made him sip, drifting on in bliss. *Heaven*, Gino said, waving a drunken arm at the sky and sea, *all the fucken boredom you could ever want.*

He began weeping once and told them all that he loved them. He asked them if they were married, had children. *Bloody oath. But this is time out from real life.* Joe, Gino and Stan were married, Joe divorced, all with grown-up children. Jim was, to Dhurgham's amazement, gay and said so exactly the same way the others said married or divorced. Jim lived with his lover, who hated the sea. Everything about their lives filled him with wonderment. He felt now and then that God had sent them as four angels in the forms of four exemplary men, examples of all he had not yet had a chance to encounter. Examples who made all ugliness into

187

beauty. Examples of everything he might have become. Angels to help him make up for lost time.

The sea was endlessly moving and still. He thought fuzzily it was as exquisite and as terrible as life, and said so. He couldn't find the words, so he used *beautiful* and *bad*. *What do you know of life?* Stan snorted indulgently, then answered himself quietly, sadly. *Probably a lot*. And Joe topped up his glass.

Dhurgham's English got better the more he drank; that of the four rough angels got worse. He stretched his legs out in the sun and felt the heat tingle and spread under his skin. His happiness bubbled inside. He licked the salt off his arm and stared at the endless sky. *You're a very good-lookin' lad*, Joe said. Dhurgham giggled and looked his warm brown legs up and down. *Yes I am*, he said.

Dhurgham felt over the memories one by one, rolling each phrase through his mind. How he loved them all, these men!

Get off that fat arse. Stan kicked at Joe but couldn't reach. He had been at the wheel a while, with Joe lounging in front of him on the deck. Joe didn't move. *Takes a big hammer to drive a big nail*, he said from under his hat. Dhurgham laughed with Stan, and Joe lifted the hat and said, *Hey, fellas, give him another—he'll be fluent soon*.

Joe taught him to sail. Dhurgham was fascinated by the GPS and the compass, the precision by which they could pinpoint their moment and place on the endless ocean. The certainty of it all.

You a virgin, Tom? Dhurgham thought for a while. He felt pure and calm. He struggled to find the English. He put his hand over his genitals. *Completely new*, he said, grinning. Joe put his hand over his own. *Past the use-by date*, he said. They all laughed. Jim told him all the mess the Australian legal system was in and what a *fuck up* its record on human rights was, *copying the crazy Americans, the Europeans, and for what?* Dhurgham told him a little bit about life in Mawirrigun but began to sob, unexpectedly, about Ammu's suicide attempt. They gave him whisky and put him to bed. It took all four of them to carry him down the gangway, giggling and cursing, and to tuck him in.

He recited to them, suddenly:

In the Name of God, the Compassionate, the Merciful. When the sun ceases to shine; when the stars fall down and the mountains are blown away—

—when camels big with young are left untended, and the wild beast are brought together; when the seas are set alight and men's souls are reunited; when the infant girl buried alive is asked for what crime she was slain; when the records of men's deeds are laid open, and heaven is stripped bare—

—when Hell burns fiercely and Paradise is brought near: then each soul shall know what it has done.

Morning Star, he said, trying to tell them, nodding seriously, his hand on his heart.

Fucken poetry, you can hear it, eh Stan? Muslim poetry.

• • •

How'd you choose us, eh, out of all the yachts at the squadron?

Dhurgham pointed to the blue *Say YES to Refugees* sticker on the coach-housing and Joe slapped his forehead. *We had the fucken* Boat Person Wanted *sign out!* As they sailed towards the Cook Strait, with Dhurgham at the helm and Joe directing him, Jim peeled it off. *Better not let them know we're mates, eh.*

They did a collection and Jim tried to stuff his shirt pockets with about six hundred dollars. But Dhurgham laughed and hugged them all, and refused. He thought that the money might make him suspect, and, more than that, he felt like a man.

He smiled sleepily. They were angels. Angels with alcohol.

See ya, Tom, in a coupla years. You'll be a Kiwi, and with a girlfriend. We'll find you. You'll be the only Assamarrai in the phone book.

Their world was so decent it was worth raging over injustice and cursing the indecent bits.

The Last Lefties on Earth.

The Ship of Fools.

The *Morning Star.*

He fell asleep in a calm that left him open.

His sleep was stalked by nightmares, each beginning and then peeling away to one that lay underneath it, until, after several layers, a dream of the red desert parted like a rotten fruit and, as if rising from dark water to become visible at the last moment,

190

the marshes appeared, threaded with mists and long slags of thin cloud. He was wading with his family in high rushes and reeds. He could hear his mother's asthmatic breathing loud in the night. She was a dark shadow behind him with a huge bundle held high and balanced on her head, giving her a grotesque silhouette. His sister was sloshing in the sodden weeds to his right, her white hijab shining dimly and her teeth flashing at him now and then, between her muttered curses. His father didn't even tell Nura off, just trudged, a shadow behind them all. He knew that his uncle and cousins were to the left, that they had fanned out for some reason. He felt excited and began to trudge with energy, despite the weight he felt sewn into his clothes. He had all their money on him; the baby, the least likely to be searched. In Syria, it would be hard, his mother said, but at least they had each other. But he was glad they had left, regardless. It was such an adventure. And there were birds in the marshes. Now and then he disturbed one and it went whirring up into the night air. He would be the first across, leading the family in a great V behind him. He was humming, lifting his legs high and squelching his sneakers vigorously into the sucking mud. He could see the darker shapes of a low rolling land ahead. He was first! He turned to Nura to say that he was going to catch the next bird that whirled away from the sedge at his feet, but Nura wasn't there. Then he heard many small noises as he faced the way they had come, noises that seemed weirdly intimate, noises of an interior, not a wide open marsh. He stood still and peered into the darkness in which nothing stood out, nothing shone. He could see nothing, and a muddy, hammering panic rose to drown him. Then he heard it, clear as a bird cry in a still night. *Run Dhurgham! Darling run!*

He woke up.

A day later he was interviewed by a tiny lady in a tight blue suit. She was accompanied by an Egyptian interpreter whose voice sounded a little like Abu Nizar's and who looked at him kindly through thick spectacles. The lady shook her head and clicked her tongue every time the interpreter repeated anything that was particularly dramatic. Dhurgham felt he was truly in a safe place, and he was quite calm throughout the interview. He pretended he had poor comprehension of English, feeling instinctively that his time in Australia tainted him, made him less the object of their concern. And listening to the interpreter paced him, gave him time to think. His dream was near and luminous and gave him courage. He hugged it close. He answered all their questions about Australia clearly. When the lady in blue tipped her head to one side like a bright bird and said gently, 'Tell us what happened that made you leave Iraq,' and the interpreter leant forward and asked the same in Arabic, he told them Aziz's story. The dream radiated in his chest. He had no doubts. He could see this story clearly too, strengthened by the one he had retrieved. For fleeting moments he could see and hear Nura and his mother in the roles he gave them. He could see the street on which he made it all unfold, his street, as he spoke.

'I and my father, mother and my sister were walking from our house to my uncle's house. Suddenly two black cars stopped beside us and just in front of us. Some men got out and told my father to get in the car. My mother grabbed his hand and stood in front of him. They told my mother that she shouldn't be on this street. My mother said, *It is my street*. The men shrugged and put us all into the cars. We were very scared.

'They took us to an empty sports stadium. There were many people there, some families, some with children. We were there all night. My father wasn't with us. They took him in the other car, and I never saw him again. We didn't talk to the other families in the stadium. We just waited through the night. I got very hungry. The next day we were told to get on three buses that had tinted windows. Soldiers were driving the buses. We were driven out of the city. Then we left the road and drove over bumpy ground into a field. There were two groups of soldiers and a bulldozer, and some other empty buses. We were ordered to get off the buses. *Hold on tight to my hands*, my mother said. One group of soldiers was pushing people into a ditch they had dug, and the other group was shooting down into the ditch. We were pushed all together to the edge. My mother said, *Recite the Shahada with me, my babies, recite the Shahada*, and she held on very tight to me. We were pushed in all together. There were many layers of bodies under me, all warm and slippery. We were near the top of the ditch. The soldiers started shooting at us but I wasn't shot. One of them pulled at my clothes and said, *This one is still alive.* They shot again, but still I wasn't shot. The bulldozer came and began to fill in the hole. It was dusk. I struggled to the edge and kept my face in some reeds so I could breathe. Then I pulled myself out of the earth, and I went to the highway. A friendly soldier stopped and picked me up and took me to my uncle's house.'

The lady in blue said little. She couldn't speak. The interpreter was sobbing.

Dhurgham felt clean. His dream was from God. He started to weep softly in his happiness. He whispered through the words of the Shahada. His mother, his father and his sister were dead—they were killed then, that suddenly, that completely, and he had always known it. God had given him Aziz's story because he was never going to be able to put his own into words.

He looked up. 'I never told this story in Australia,' he said in a firm voice. 'I was too young. I couldn't remember it clearly enough but I can now.'

• • •

Dhurgham remained three weeks in remand in Wellington with no news, then was released pending the outcome of the refugee determination process. He knew nothing more. He was met by Mr Johns, who smiled tiredly and told him that he would be billeted with the Johns family until his result was announced.

He looked at Mr Johns and smiled too, uncertain, grateful. He got into the car and watched New Zealand flit by. The shift was far shorter than the sudden journey from Mawirrigun to Kanugo Kagil, but he felt the same dislocation, as if his body had been taken somewhere and his mind and soul, caught out playing truant, found themselves left behind and having to follow on foot.

What he didn't know was that a powerful lobby group had got hold of the facts of his story and had demanded his release in accordance with the usual treatment of convention claimants. Mr Harwood had said all hostels were full, while consulting frantically with a team of legal advisers. Mr Johns, pushed by Janine, had offered to billet him and earned a filthy look from Mr Harwood and a direct accusation of being the 'leak'. Dhurgham was still not released. A week later it was in the media in Australia and New Zealand, and the next day Dhurgham was out. He was New Zealand's darling. Mr Harwood told Mr Johns that he could forget ever being promoted and, if any evidence surfaced that he had spoken to the media on classified matters, he would be sacked without accrued benefits.

'And keep that walking disaster away from the media, you hear?'

Mr Johns was silent.

Mr Harwood had a private meeting with the Prime Minister. Australia was in the process of signing billions in trade contracts and it was a bad time for New Zealand to say that Australia was an oppressive regime. As Dhurgham was released, Mr Harwood was on the phone to Mr Cowell, AID Minister in Canberra, in damage control. He got a cool reception and had to fight uphill to convince the Australians that he wanted what they did. 'Of course he is not being treated as a convention claimant!' he said. 'The idea is ludicrous. We have him held at the residence of one of our officers until we can resolve this matter at law and to *your* satisfaction. You know what these lobby groups are like—don't pay any attention to the papers.'

'Dig! Dig!' Mr Harwood yelled at his team. 'We've got to find something. This can't be happening. Ask AID for his entire case history, off the record. They're as keen to resolve this as we are.'

Carrie Johns met Dhurgham with open hostility. She looked him up and down with seventeen year old righteousness, turned to Janine and said loud enough for him to hear, 'He looks like a terrorist.'

'Carrie!'

But for some reason Dhurgham didn't feel shy. He was bursting, his chest full, body charged. He felt like hugging himself. He felt like raising his arms to the sky to hold the charge at his furthermost. He was more than grateful to the Johns, and exceedingly polite, but he suddenly felt too big and too free to go through the door into their house.

'Please, Mrs Johns, may I—?' he gestured towards the green garden.

'Carrie, show Thor—him the garden.' Janine had a warning note in her voice and Dhurgham felt like laughing out loud. Nothing mattered. He felt so much older than Carrie. And he felt in love with Carrie. He walked with a spring at an appropriate distance from her, wanting to run. She sulked next to him, waving her hand at this and that in the garden, not saying a word. He watched her fine arms flung this way and that, her long fingers with black nail polish. He caught the scent of her shining black hair, pulled back in a ponytail. A sort of teenage, apple and peach scent, a waft he almost recognised. A young, free smell. Her breasts were small and high under her tight shirt. Her face was triangular, pointy and aggressive. Her shiny black hair flicked back and forth across a broad white brow. Her eyes were large, dark and right now very nasty. He wanted to laugh. He leant towards her slightly and looked at her, his eyes shining, until she unwillingly met his glance.

'Hey, New Zealand! Have you ever met a terrorist before?'

And then he could not stop himself from running, his arms in the air. It was an impossibly green garden. He ran down the long lawn-like meadow towards the looming ferns, trees and green belt that bordered a hidden stream that wound through the garden. He was laughing, his body bursting, his skin singing, the charge reaching the sky. His feet seemed to press an aroma from the grass and earth: herbs, flowers and cut grass, crushed grass, and underneath it all—wet earth. He didn't look back until he reached the bottom, a small semicircle of brighter green grass forming a thick mat on the bank of the creek. He could not sit. Carrie was stomping down the slope after him. She came up alongside.

'This is my spot. You are trespassing.'

Dhurgham grinned. He didn't understand.

Carrie pointed at the ground. 'Mine!' She pointed at him and said very slowly, insultingly, 'Illegal immigrant.'

Dhurgham pointed at her and said, equally slowly, 'Bitch.'

Carrie stared at him, her eyes widening in shock. She spun and raced up the hill to the house, leaving him there. Dhurgham stared down the steep, fern covered embankment. He could see a glimmer of a forest pool down there. If it wasn't for the tree trunks and the furry fern trunks, one might have run down the grassy slope and jumped, flying through the air, to land in that still black water. His elation had left him. He felt himself quieten, retreat from the sky, the trees and the grass, and re-enter his body. He probably should not insult the daughter of his hosts but, although his high joy had left him, he was not regretful. Not now.

'He called me a bitch!' Carrie was outraged. They were doing him a huge favour. Her dad had nearly lost his job for this guy. He was in their house, for God's sake, out of the kindness of their hearts.

Janine laughed, although she was slightly taken aback.

'What did you call him?'

'An illegal immigrant, which is what he is.'

'And a terrorist.'

'Most likely ditto. Australia rejected him, remember.'

'Pretty bitchy, Carrie.'

'But shouldn't he be quiet and grateful and stuff, and generally more, more—'

'Subservient?'

'Yes! He is trying to get into the country for nothing!'

'Maybe that's not him. Maybe that's what got him into trouble in Australia.'

Carrie swung her hair in irritation and went to her room. She sat on her bed, then went to her window and watched Dhurgham walk slowly back through the rhododendrons and hydrangeas up towards the house. He didn't look crushed. He stood up straight. His hair was wet, as though he had run his hands in the creek water and then slicked them through it, and his eyebrows looked like birds' wings. He was dark and shining against the pale pink of the bunched flowers.

Dhurgham settled into the Johns household quickly. He loved their house. It was made of wood and built into a steep slope so that the street face and the front looking over the huge garden both seemed in different ways to be the front. It was timber, outside and in. The floor was polished a pale golden colour and all the walls were cream. It was light and airy throughout. The kitchen was part of a long open room with colourful rugs on the floor, a lounge and TV, and a dining table. Sunlight seemed to fill this room nearly all day through a series of floor-to-ceiling windows that looked north and out over the garden below. His room had a bay window facing west; Carrie's had an identical window facing east. Outside his window the rhododendrons massed, and in the middle distance the mountain rose sharply, peppered with many variations of the same kind of stately yet modest house. The sky, usually either blanketed or speckled with clouds, filled one triangle of his compound window. He loved it all.

Carrie told him that he was not to go near the bathroom until after 8.30 am, do anything male with the toilet seat, or to wander the house in his pyjamas, so he didn't. Janine gave him a set of keys as his own and told him with an indulgent smile to try not to lose them. He treasured them, amused and charmed by the typical teenager her smile made him out to be. He read books in their library, watched whatever television programs they watched, washed the dishes after dinner (earning an approving comment from Janine and a filthy look from Carrie). Janine gave him a razor and a can of shaving lotion and his own set of shampoo, conditioner, toothpaste and toothbrush. He shaved his face for the novelty of it rather than the necessity and made sure he left no chin or lip hair in the bathroom that might annoy Carrie. He made his bed every day and learnt how to use a front-loader washing machine. He lay in his bed at night, reading, then just staring at his cedar door. It had scrolls, waves and polished ridges of red running through the deep maroon brown. It gleamed. He loved it that his door and Carrie's across the hallway were the same style but each unique in its swirls and wood patterns.

Dhurgham's new land was new the way no other had been. He was free to discover it, to find where he had finally landed, where he would, one day, be at home. He took to walking everywhere through

Wellington's startling city scape. It was a hilly city, a city that hadn't fitted into the small harbour bay and had flowed up the steep mountains and over into the many steep valleys and clefts. From the Johns' it was an hour's walk to the harbour city, a walk that took him through the suburbs over small winding village roads to peaks bristling with cute whitewashed wooden houses overlooking stunning views of the sea and mountains. He thought, in that first week, that it was the loveliest place he had ever seen, and the thought filled him with an inexplicable pain and lone-liness, even foreboding.

The first time he headed over the peaks to the final steep descent from the cottages to the skyscrapers was full of surprise. He found himself faced with woodland, or parkland, rather than houses. He plunged down into what was suddenly no park, but a thick forest. Its smell hit him: thick, fecund, rotted. He could hear water gurgling and singing; a wild brook, no fountain. He stared up at the tangled trees, lianas and ferns. He had never seen anything so majestic in its excess. Gnarled roots tripped him as he strode. Huge dark trunks, most of them tagged with tiny plastic markers giving a number, rose to make the kind of forest canopy he had only ever seen in movies. It was utterly silent, as if wild enough to have hushed at his entrance.

A few metres down the track, he heard the sizzling sound he later found out was cicadas. And then the forest was ticking and wheezing, sighing and twittering in his ears. At first it was just the sigh and creak of wood on wood, leaves against each other, and the sudden soft thud of a pine cone falling. Then simple notes, then complex scrapes and whistles of a bird. And suddenly he found he could hear a child playing somewhere, a sound that must have been there before. It was a loose scuffling on a parallel track, hidden somewhere to his left. He could tell a child was shooting an imaginary enemy with limited success, making attack after attack with increasing bravery. A woman was laughing. He smiled to himself.

Then, behind the unfamiliar bird calls and the fading gunshots, he heard a distant squeak and thwock that he took to be another strange creature. But as the path rounded a bend, the forest gave way suddenly to a view through trees of green asphalt tennis courts way below in the valley. Small figures, girls in white shirts and short blue skirts, ran back and forth. The path turned back into the deep green shadows and he strode on under the giant umbrellas of tree ferns. Again there was no real sign that he was in a city until the steep path gave way to garden as it levelled at the bottom. *Central Park*, the sign said.

There was nothing on earth he had ever imagined to be like New Zealand.

Dinner at the Johns' was a slightly formal affair in which everyone who was in the house, family or friends, gathered to give due appreciation to Janine's cooking; to be given also, in excess, when Carrie cooked. It was a subtle ritual that Dhurgham understood without thought. He passed his comment, too, on each dish. He participated lightly in political discussions and generally carried himself as a young man who respected his elders. He felt completely at ease at these dinners. He looked forward to them. He could feel the approval of Mr Johns and Janine. He could feel their guests' interest in him as a kind of generosity and he knew that they left impressed by him. And he could feel Carrie writhe and snarl under her calm face. With all this he felt at ease, relaxed and natural.

Carrie cracked, finally, after three weeks. The family were gathered over a spaghetti bake she had made, which was overcooked. She had planned all morning to make something special and had shopped especially for unusual ingredients: artichoke hearts and aubergine. She was furious with everyone for the blackened tips of the spaghetti, the mush underneath and the hardness of the browned crust. She smacked the salad bowl down on the table slightly too hard and sat down to eat without a word. A tear slid down her cheek and she kept her head down.

'Hmmm—good!' Dhurgham said.

Carrie raised her fierce face to his and said, 'Mr …
Perfect!'

Without thought Dhurgham flicked a cherry tomato across the table at her and hit her on the cheek. Carrie gasped, and then, despite herself, despite everything, she smiled. She began looking for something to throw back.

'Kids! Kids!' Janine laughed. 'Settle down!'

Carrie kicked Dhurgham under the table and they grinned at each other.

Carrie bought Dhurgham a watch as a present. She spent all her saved pocket money that was not in her term account. She showed Janine in the car as they arrived home from shopping. Her mother raised an eyebrow at her and Carrie blushed.

'He hasn't got a watch,' she said softly.

'It's really nice Carrie—help to make up for how rude you were to him when you first met.'

Carrie blushed again and slammed the car door. She stormed into the house and threw it at him, scowling. It hit him in the chest.

Dhurgham was stunned. He held the small blue-wrapped box in both hands. Carrie leant in close with a little impatient dance. 'Open it!'

He could smell her hair.

It was a most beautiful watch—solid and silver, exactly the kind of watch, he thought, that he might have chosen for himself. Carrie grabbed it from him and put it around his wrist, where its segments settled, smooth and cool. He fingered the shining glass, admiring the fine filigree of the hands and their stately movement over the reflective blue base beneath.

He was smiling broadly. 'Thank you!' he murmured, raising his eyes to hers. She glowed back for a moment and then shrugged away, buoyant.

'It's a Sentinel,' she said, and he guessed from her nonchalance that this meant a lot.

Janine watched them from the kitchen, troubled. How could she blame Carrie? Tom was such a lovely boy. She hoped John was right that Tom would win his case. She hoped they were all right that Tom was what he seemed to be.

Dhurgham looked at Carrie uncomfortably. She was right. He could go to school next year, if—if. Then he could go to university. But it all seemed unreal. Carrie was his age. Carrie had just finished school and was taking a year off, a notion that had at first struck him as comical, then blissfully bizarre. Carrie was in her *year off*. She was *choosing* to have some time out of the flow of life. Then she was going to university. He sat up, staring away over the creek and into the wild lush mountainside. A tui called, grating and liquid notes

hidden in the shadowed green. Panic crept out of the
wilds and gripped him. His education! Life had slid on,
slipped away, leaving him stranded. He had his twelve
year old precocity, *Oh Master Dhurgham, you can be
anything, anything in the world you want to be, with that
mind. You only have to do your homework.* He had had
ten months with Abu Rafik with which to become an
adult, but the world hadn't waited for him. Carrie, next
to him, Carrie in her frilly yellow tank top, with long
brown legs and jandals. Carrie slouching and pet-
ulant and elegant with it. She had kept up. Carrie had
his story.

'I think I'll be a pilot, though,' Carrie said
suddenly, and the hair on Dhurgham's neck stood
on end.

Carrie was delighted at first by everything that was
different about Dhurgham. He noticed birds. She had
never seen so many birds as she did in his company.
She told him the antics of keas and the way they
would tease a dog, and he laughed and laughed. She
said she had to show him one of these quirky green
parrots, hopping along the kerb, 'looking for cars to
trash,' she said. But there were none around
Wellington. She promised to take him when she got
her licence.

'Look, birds!' she would scream, poking him, and he would look, stop, and regard them, face serious. She loved it. She loved him when he did it.

He didn't tell her that he didn't remember having been interested in birds before—that his interest in birds increased with her amusement. His interest was real nonetheless; and he felt perhaps it was proper that such an interest should surface here. For a while he thought that knowing birds and plants, naming them, knowing all there was to know about them, would bond him into place. He would find his place among them. 'I'll be a New Zealander when I know all this,' he said, 'serious.' Carrie laughed witheringly. She didn't have to say it. Carrie knew neither the names nor habits nor calls of any birds. She could recognise a tui and knew that magpies had come over from Australia, but her answers were vague on everything else—'Oh those—yeah, you hear them all the time.'

Nonetheless, birds charmed him.

They were lying together on the grass at the bottom of the garden, staring up into the fern fronds and the spreading canopy of the late-flowering pohutakawa. It was one of those rare days when the aromatic grass was dry enough to lie on. 'It's a completely different world up there,' he said. Silver-eyes and sparrows flitted back and forth. 'We live like this.' He made a flat palm and pushed it horizontally, then in a mechanical line left, a line right. 'Birds live like this.' He reached his arms up and made a sphere, then a radiating ball, an explosion of possibility. Then he said softly, 'In the war I remember all the birds died. Even the flies. Stunned out of the sky by the blasts. There were dead birds all over the garden every morning.'

Carrie frowned. She propped herself up on her elbow to look at him. A war could be out there, impending somewhere far away, or talked about by someone from a war coming to class, but she didn't want to be trapped with someone with a war in their memories, someone who saw all the birds fall from the sky. Then she felt scared.

'My father was in a war, too, in Vietnam, but *he* never talks about it,' she said.

Skipper Joe was behind him, guiding his hand now and then at the helm.

'Firm, but gentle, gentle, young fella. Feel it out. The wind and the current aren't made to work for you, they're out there, wild and changeable as all get-out. You got to feel out the pathway that makes music on them.'

The *Morning Star* cut in and hissed into smooth sea. The sails snapped and trilled.

'Nope … yes, nearly nearly! Just a little more, and then keep feeling for it. It's like pleasuring a woman. It's all there already. Know what I mean?'

'No,' Dhurgham said shyly, smiling, glancing at Joe's grizzled face and bare dome of a head.

Joe smiled. 'You're off again, back, back, yep ... That's it. See the sails, no little creases and ripples in the wrong spots. Feel it?'

'Yes,' murmured Dhurgham without shifting his concentration from the wheel, the boat and the sea. Joe was silent.

Dhurgham could feel the warmth of Joe's sunny body just behind him, and hear his breath moving back and forth through a smile. He held his concentration, but it suddenly was no effort. It was a dreamy balanced dance.

'It's like finding your future. It's fate, and all there, but shit ya can fuck it up.' Joe was silent for a moment, then his voice settled lower, softer, near Dhurgham's ear. 'I was in a war once. With him.' He waved at Stan's feet hanging over the coach-housing. 'We went to Vietnam as young fellas. I was so young and stupid I kinda ... thrived. Can't bear to think about it now. Those other two were protesting against us for all they were worth. Jim even got put in prison. I think they tapped his phone up until the 80s. Keep feeling for it, know what I mean?'

Dhurgham wasn't sure whether Joe meant fate or the course of the *Morning Star*. He didn't know what to say. The boat then dug and slowed, and the sails snapped as he handed the wheel back.

Carrie got her full driver's licence in a flurry of excitement and celebration in the Johns' household.

The Tararua mountains were cloud-wet. They set up camp in a soggy clearing surrounded by the black trunks and filigree fronds of tree ferns. They were perched above a hundred metre drop to a river that rushed and roared through boulders and stilled into clear green pools. They could see them way below but couldn't even reach them with far-flung stones.

As night fell, the pines and ferns raised a dim blue-black canopy over their heads and the sentinel trunks flickered orange in the light of their campfire.

Carrie had reassured him that, no, there were no snakes, no tigers, no dogs. Not even foxes—only birds and small insects. No large insects, except wetas, and she said that so dismissively that he assumed they were some hidden away, unobtrusive burrower.

It had taken a good two hours for his nerves to settle, with Carrie laughing at what a city boy he was, and teasing him about kiwis and their long beaks. He had never slept outside in the wilds like this. Carrie didn't let up, but he could tell that her deft expertise and joyous authority were enhanced by his inexperience. When he asked her how often she camped out, her answer was airy with superiority and he smiled to himself. He trusted her utterly, entrusted himself to her. It didn't matter that she hadn't done this much. He was guessing that she had camped with her parents. It mattered only that she knew about the *idea* of camping, that she knew what things were for, what one did at night, that the idea of camping formed part of her imagination, part of who she was and would be in her lifetime. That was more wonderful and more essential than any real experience.

Carrie set him to work gathering wood, preparing toasting sticks, opening the corn, holding tent poles, and helping zip the two sleeping bags together.

Later they sat huddled together in the double sleeping bag on the groundsheet by the fire, giggling as they ate the dreadful mush of eggs, corn and beef they had cooked. Dhurgham settled into wonder and happiness, the glory of the world before his eyes in the glowing coals, in the far starlight, in Carrie's lithe body resting against him. The stars and crescent moon had faint haloes. He felt the glory of the world rushing on the night air into his lungs with every breath. He held Carrie tighter. She breathed deeply, snuggled in close, then stunned him.

'Do you want sex?' she asked.

'No!' Dhurgham almost leapt up in shock. He was jolted to the core, and the alien night suddenly assaulted him. He couldn't get away.

'Oh,' Carrie said in a small voice, and wrapped her arms about her knees. They were locked shoulder to shoulder.

The outrageous question seeped through Dhurgham despite himself and he couldn't get it out of his head. The word sank through to his heart and belly, and down to his cock and thrummed over and over. Sex. Sex. Sex. He didn't want to touch Carrie, he didn't want to have sex with Carrie, not now, but he wanted to have sex. His body was alive with it. He wanted at least to take her hand and put it where she would feel his desire. He closed his eyes, wondering, wondering about Carrie. Western girls. His groin pulsed and ached and his penis pressed painfully against his underclothes.

He thought of Mr Hosni and his desire ebbed away, leaving him feeling gross and nasty. He wanted words now, confessions, not touch. He wanted to know everything.

After a little while, he couldn't stop himself from asking, 'How many—?'

Carrie spun on, him, glancing at him with a stabbing look, then turned away. 'Oh! Never! Sorry I asked.' Her eyes were angry, embarrassed. She tossed her head furiously and glowered at the fire, and Dhurgham saw a tear run down her cheek, leaving a shining gold trail. His heart twisted then, and both his joy and the glory of the world returned with a rush. He wrapped his arms around her, squeezing until he felt her ribs bend. She gasped, laughing, and kissed his hair.

'I love you!' His voice was taut with pain. Carrie sucked in her breath, and her eyes shone as she caught him in a full, swift, sideways glance.

'That's good!' She thought for a moment, then laughed. '"Do you want sex?" What a way to start your sex life!'

'You always give me things that way,' he said eventually, feeling humbled. 'You hit me with them.'

Dhurgham listened to the crackle of the fire and the rush of the river far below them. Then something ticked and scraped closer, somewhere on his arm. He saw the wild filaments of long antennae first, and, scalp crawling, he gingerly pulled his loose sleeve towards the light. He screamed, shrieked, as the giant carapace lurched on his arm. He leapt up, snatched a burning stick and beat it from him in one fluid violent move. The beast was flung across the fire into the darkness as Dhurgham caught a whiff of an unimaginable filthy smell. He stood, heaving and shuddering, staring out after it. Carrie pulled him down beside her, laughing herself almost sick.

'Weta!' she gasped.

And that was all it took.

In Dhurgham's memory this night, like that other, stood out. This Dhurgham, like his proud twelve year old self in the marshes carrying his family's wealth, this was himself at his maximum. It was what might have been. And he felt pinned precariously to a place and time on Carrie's body and on the spinning world.

They giggled and knocked knees like children, undressing themselves and each other while trying to keep the sleeping bag up. They paused only a moment, once they were naked, staring at each other with glee. Then they shuffled awkwardly together, until Dhurgham reached his arms around Carrie's smooth sides, down, and wrapped both hands under her buttocks, pulling her towards him, reeling with the heat and wetness of her running over his fingers. Carrie hitched the sleeping bag awkwardly to her shoulder, twisting to keep it up on them both, and reached with her other hand for his penis. She laughed, gleaming darkly at him from under her fringe. He moaned as she kissed him, hard, then harder. They were clumsy lovers. Carrie frowned at him, and said 'Ouch!' so accusingly that she had to kiss him again to unfreeze him. They were very quick lovers. It was over soon after the ouch. But Dhurgham remembered Carrie gleaming and warm and white-silver *with him*, stark and soft under the moonlight as the mountain dripped and sang around them. In his memory it was endless. He remembered the moment of shining release, in which Carrie arched in his hands, calling to him across the sky, her hands pulling at his thighs as he pushed into her beyond himself and her. They were every lover, they were young and the first, and they were as old as honey. In that moment he was empty and full, and everything was hope and glory and terror but he was the living body of freedom.

Carrie was elated to have done it. She felt mysterious, felt the exciting pull of adulthood. When she got home, a day later, she rushed to her room. She swayed her sinewy body at the mirror and glowered at herself. The image of Dhurgham naked rose again and again in her mind.

She remembered the surprise of hot sweaty skin sticking against her in the sleeping bag afterwards as the air chilled to freezing on their faces. She had been afraid for a moment that theirs was a precarious perch, and that a landslide would rip them from the mountainside and bury them in a pile of mud and rocks way below in the river. She had worried that she hadn't told her parents where they would camp, and that even her body might be lost forever. Now she was glad. He was hers and sex hadn't hurt much.

She had dated and furiously dropped a succession of boyfriends and was suddenly, now, curious about their bodies. Were they as beautiful as Tom? Did their nipples harden with their dark, musky cocks? Did they have the same smooth soft skin over firm stomachs? They would each be different, whiter, darker, stronger, weaker. Tom smelt good. Like saltwater and sunshine. What did men smell like?

She wanted to worry and tease her mother, but

was shocked by Janine's surprise. Janine turned to her daughter, face clouded.

'I didn't realise, Carrie—'

'That I liked Tom?'

'No. I thought … Greg, Darren, Ewan—'

'Oh.'

'At the end of school I'm off to Whistler, Canada!' Darren punched the air in a victory grab. 'Skiiing! Snowboarding!'

'I could ski!' Dhurgham said eagerly. 'I will go with you!'

Darren looked at him, then smiled.

'You being a refugee, Tom, you wouldn't be able to travel. You'll be living on handouts until a taxi company takes you. And that's only if they decide to let you stay.'

The others looked at Darren, shuffling but not disputing it.

'What?' Darren looked around, his hands held palms out, shoulders up. 'I'm only saying the truth. What?'

Carrie leapt forward, between him and Dhurgham, facing the semicircle of the others.

'Tom's been all over the world,' she said, haughtily. 'He's been to—' she held up her hand in Darren's face and, starting with her little finger, bent each finger down, as if to deal with a country once and for all, bring it to its knees. 'Eye-Rak, Syria, Indo-nesia, Australia, and—' she waggled the thumb until it, too, capitulated, 'New Zealand.'

She tossed her short black hair and flashed a dark look at Dhurgham. *That showed them*, her look said, and Dhurgham's discomfort melted away. Countries just folded under Carrie's fingertips. He was more charmed than he could say by her defence of him, and by her easy dismissal of countries. He felt a lump rise in his throat. She would too! *Iraq, (or Eye-rak!) been there, done that*, she'd say. No one would dare to touch her, because she had her confidence, her father and her country behind her. How powerful Carrie and how powerless Dhurgham! He looked down at his finely muscled arm, his wrist and hand (like his mother's but bigger). He glanced at Carrie's long white fingers threaded between each of his dark ones. He felt a wave of possessiveness, need and envy all at once.

A person should travel, see the world and return. Bring home impressions, jokes, experiences, and the richness of knowing themselves and their special place in the world. He sat alone in the garden, later, trying to think about what Carrie had said. He housed so many lives, not visits. Iraq was home, but was imaginary, lost in his child-hood. Syria. In Syria he was someone else, someone no member of his family could have known or recognised. Indonesia. Yes, just two weeks, but Indonesia itself floated evanescent on that solid ocean, that scored deck and the stale breath of boys. He had lived a whole man's life from youth to old age and the end of all things on that ocean. Twelve days as big as fifty years.

Australia. In Australia he never quite found either the calm horror of the boat or the confusion of what went before. He had never found the stillness-in-fear or the glory of the mosaic. In Australia he never caught up with himself. In Australia he imagined himself into many selves, but never Syria, never Iraq. In Australia he waited for life but didn't live it. And he never really saw Australia. Mr Jean-Luc's sweet smile floated up. Australians *were* good. They had shown it. Mr Peter had helped him by worrying about him and harrying him. Mr Jean-Luc had helped him. His rights had mattered to Mr Jean-Luc. And Joyce Collyer and Robin Tucker. They had cared about him in principle, without even knowing him. Then *time out from real life*. His angels. They had helped him by liking him and that was the most important of all. A short sail seemingly to the end of all things, to happiness, but he turned and took the long murky path, yes, he did, New Zealand, because he had not yet begun a life that took him beyond twelve. He punched the grass rhythmically and pulled at the roots of his hair, unaware that he was doing it. Each place was wrapped up like the body of a young martyr, each buried away from the others. He had no choice but to walk away from his own death, over and over again, and try to start again elsewhere, each time sealing off the dead hope behind him.

He had housed too many shifts with no return, like a scientist who has subjected himself to too many unnatural experiments. And each had thinned him, left him more remote from himself and the world. He felt sere and brittle. Old. He remembered his grandfather suddenly; saw with the clarity that he had not had as a twelve year old—an old man who would not move from his field in Samarra and the graves of his loves no matter the danger. But he, Dhurgham, had no graves to tie him to life. No person can go through so many possible lives and live none of them! Tears of rage welled from his eyes and he threw handfuls of grass and soil at New Zealand's alien grey sky.

'You are home!' he screamed in an adolescent voice cracking with disbelief and fear.

'Dhurgham,' he said. '*Dturr—ghaam*. It means young lion.'

'Thergrarm … Dergram,' Carrie tried. She looked as though she was tasting a new food with uncertain expectations. He could see straight away that she would never say it as his name—only as an exotic item he had brought with him to show her. She frowned at his silence.

'I can't do it, Tom. I'd feel silly trying. Tom's a sweet name, isn't it?'

Carrie's face was quiet and sad. She was thinking about how much it annoyed her when friends heard Tom call her Kiri or Curry or even something that sounded like Kelly. She tossed her hair back as unexpected tears started in her eyes. She decided to be proud of all of them (except Curry).

He kissed her. He would be Tom. After everything, how could this little thing matter?

Iraq. Feeling nasty, he had deliberately offended Carrie and her friend Samantha. He hadn't liked Samantha. She looked young and pretty. She giggled. She breathed 'Ya gotta be joking!' when he said he was Iraqi.

'What was your name again?' he asked, although he had heard it clearly.

'Samantha. Do you like it?' and she raised her happy face to him, waiting for the sure affirmative.

He was silent, itching with an obscure anger.

'I would,' he said, 'but that is what we call low-class women in my country.'

Carrie glared at him and dropped her jaw stagily in a gesture of disgust and disbelief. She also looked young and carefree, free to be revolted by him. He felt vaguely pleased in a twisted, miserable way. She had given him a withering look and had taken the shocked Samantha off. She said something over her shoulder at him that he didn't hear. He heard the last bit—'no wonder they're going to bomb it to shit.'

He stood alone in the mall, suddenly tired. He knew nothing, really, of Iraq. It was a dream. He couldn't say, haughtily, *Well, where I come from* ... as the definitive measure for all things right and proper. He found he couldn't remember much of what was about to be bombed. Just a night sky, a nightmare, a street, a video of himself and the scent of his room. Populated by his mother, his sister, his father. Ammu. No, Ammu was Australia, lost in a hospital. He couldn't stand on his roots, mobilise his own country against anyone, because it was so long gone, and he was a man now, not a boy. Somehow he hadn't brought it with him.

It took him a while to make up with Carrie. He knocked on her door, knowing she was in; then, when there was no answer, he pushed it open. She was sitting cross-legged on her bed, looking like a jinniya from a storybook. The pressure of her glower kept him near the door.

'Well?' she said, after the silence had gone on so long that she knew he wasn't going to break it. He stuck his hands deep into his pockets and glared back. 'Samantha was disgusted. And *freaked out*. And she'll tell everyone.'

He shrugged and stayed leaning against the wall. Carrie narrowed her eyes at him, then hopped sideways, smiled, and gestured for him to sit next to her. He sauntered over, secretly charmed and relieved.

Carrie's room always intrigued him. They were sitting on her single bed with its fresh white sheets and patchwork quilt. An array of cute objects were set on the sill and dresser and stuck to the walls. The walls had posters pinned on them at crooked angles. One was of a guitarist caught screaming in dark smoke with sparks coming from his fingers; another of a girl with long black hair swirling over almost naked breasts and thighs. She had pearlescent skin, a tiny mouth, v-shaped chin, floppy fringe and impossibly huge liquid eyes. Another picture was of a near-naked airbrushed youth with a hairless chest. His giant brown eyes smouldered above his elfin chin. His underpants showed above his jeans. A herd of gazelles leapt in a purple middle-distance behind him.

The pictures made Dhurgham uncomfortable but Carrie having them in her room fascinated him.

Carrie's smell was in everything. He buried his nose suddenly in her pillow, rubbing his head over her quilt, and she laughed. He came up grinning. He felt much better.

'You girls have everything,' he said, not meaning it as a criticism.

Carrie flared. 'I worked for that, you know.' She pointed to her stereo. 'I paid for it after working all summer. Not like the girls in Iraq—probably not even allowed to get jobs.'

He thought about it. His thoughts were all happy and inchoate. He couldn't explain what he meant.

On sudden impulse he slid off the bed and lifted the valance.

Carrie screamed, 'What are you doing?'

He started hauling stuff out from under her bed as she tried to push it back. Then she began to help, until they had a relatively tidy pile of bears, dolls, makeup, pictures, broken electrical soft toys, books and a box full of tiny clothes. Carrie was fingering things lovingly, familiarly.

'Why do you put these things here?' He was holding up a grimy blue-eyed doll with about twenty tiny iridescent hairclips in its hair.

'They are little-girl stuff,' she said.

He pulled the clothes out of the box. Carrie giggled.

'They are some of my favourite baby clothes. Mum gave them to me. My girl clothes are all here.' And she patted the patchwork quilt. Carrie had been a stylish baby. Yellow butterfly buttons, ladybug suits, a cute green space alien on a tiny black T-shirt. He folded them reverently and packed them back in the box. He tidied her toys carefully and laid them back under her bed. He sat down next to her.

'Sorry for pissing off your friends.'

'Well, Sam will never come on to you, at least.'
They laughed.

Dhurgham stood at the doorway of the softly lit room. The white linen curtains were drawn, giving Mr and Mrs Johns' room a golden glow in the midmorning light. The bed was tousled; mountains of tumbled lace and cream doona, soft and rubbed, maybe still warm. Pictures and tapestries of shepherds and European trees hung on the pale pink walls but Dhurgham paid them no attention. He was breathing deeply, drawing in the stale fug of the room. The sweat, easy farts and overused bed. The fug of parents. He was sweating suddenly, in his yearning, in the memory of a cloudy scent that was not here but might have been. He had a sense of his own limbs as small and smooth, tucked into big, warm, smelly arms. He reeled with it for a moment. He suddenly imagined Mr and Mrs Johns having sex, tossing and creaking on that same bed in front of him. Their bellies loose and straining, their hands practised, their smells so familiar to them they were unnoticeable, known to the point of being unknown. Dhurgham stood there watching, breathing deeply, savouring their sex, imagining its ordinariness, its ease. And slowly, as his cock rose, he became miserable with a confusion mixed with something twisting his heart in a vice.

He was envious. He could never creep back into the right path to a real life. He turned away from the fog that hung in their empty room, hating now its stale stink of other, faraway lives. He shut his eyes as he leant back against the wall, rubbing himself hard to drown out his misery in his own rhythm.

Dhurgham, Carrie, Tim and Julie were in McDonalds. Tim had a black eye. Carrie touched it with a fingertip and winced elaborately in sympathy.

'I got jumped out the back of the Te Aro service station. It was really scary. They had a van, and they were speaking Allah this and Allah that, AllaAkba when they punched me.'

Tim leant in, glancing at Dhurgham, 'It was al Qaeda, in *Wellington*. Darren already told me that they had a cell here.'

Dhurgham leant back, shaking his head, pursing his lips thoughtfully until he had their attention.

'Nope,' he said. 'Wasn't us.'

Carrie stared at the shocked faces and shrieked with laughter, pointing at Tim and Julie, hooting in glee. She mimed shooting both of them. Julie and Tim smiled slowly, uncertainly. Dhurgham glowed.

Dhurgham didn't like Carrie's friends. He noticed their easygoing banter and their light cruelty with each other and couldn't smile. They used their opinions on music to compete and humiliate. He imagined them surfing the net late into the night, giggling over porn sites. He imagined them in a chatroom with Mr Hosni, who was, after all, only a URL away. His guts twisted painfully. What if Mr Hosni had broken that promise and there were images of *him*? Would they recognise him? He sat with them, awash with rage and shame.

Carrie's friends hated the Prime Minister. The woman in power in Enzed, the woman who would uphold human rights, the woman who would save him, was at their mercy—they were all voting for the first time in their lives soon.

'She looks like a horse,' Julie said.

'She hates hip-hop,' Tim said witheringly. 'She hasn't got the guts to say it outright.'

Tim and Darren began arguing about the achievements of Elemenopop and Scribe.

Dhurgham's confidence faltered.

Personal details, he thought. *Full Name: Dhurgham Mohammad Amer Hassan As-Samarra'i. Nickname: Terrorist. (Angel. Birdie.)*

Married: to educated New Zealand national. No children.

Education: Primary, seven years in Madrasat al Maamoun, Karrada, Baghdad, Iraq. 42 months in Mawirrigun Aliens Processing Centre, Mawirrigun, Central Gumuny Australia. Graduated and went on a yacht cruise to New Zealand.

Skills: Art. Insulting people. Languages. Rebuilding myself in new countries with less and less rather than more and more.

Interests: Love. Truth. Beauty. Wisdom. Survival. Flame. Rose. Dagger. Heart. The Past. Also I like birds.

Hopes …

Hopes.

Mr Johns gave Dhurgham a page from the *Dominion Post*.

'That yacht you were on. It sank! Lucky you got off in time, aye.'

Dhurgham took the paper, his hands shaking. The *Morning Star* was there in a colour photo, with Skipper Joe smiling through his beard at the camera. Underneath there were small square photos of Joe,

Jim, Stan and Gino. He could barely recognise them. He couldn't read it. He didn't need to. *He had always known*. A wave of numbness crashed into him and stayed. He felt the turn then. His life jibed, keel biting, and caught a different wind.

'I wish I was with them,' he said.

'Asshole,' said Carrie and left the room.

Janine and John Johns exchanged worried glances. *He certainly lied about that yacht*, Mr Johns thought, and looked at Dhurgham with new mistrust. But Janine sat down and put her arm round Dhurgham, who hunched, oversized, awkward, in her embrace.

'You are a cruel one, John,' she said later.

He was broken, wires raw and snipped, flaring unexpectedly with memories, seared by them.

Mr Hosni was back with his soft, clean fingers, parting and probing. Dhurgham's body was marked by those old touches, here and here; and through the marks Mr Hosni could return any time and unclench Dhurgham's crooked fingers from the world. Mr Hosni was a gatekeeper, and Carrie was a phantom, a dream. Dhurgham lay in bed sweating and numb.

Mr Hosni did nothing. He sat on the edge of the bed. He chatted through the night, reminding

Dhurgham of the good times; looking, to Dhurgham's eye, a little old and sad.

'Remember when we went to Busra? You loved it. You even forgot your family for a while and were as happy as any child should be. I was happy seeing you happy. I loved you, Birdie. I gave you everything I had.'

'That's a terrible lie,' Dhurgham croaked weakly.

'No,' said Mr Hosni, 'it's the truth. In any case, it's my truth. I'm a bad man, but I am proud of myself for what I did for you. And I sent you to Australia to a new life with more than enough money to get you started, more than I ever gave anybody, even my own mother. What do you think would have happened to you if I hadn't taken you in and educated you myself? Do you think even Peter Pan and Wendy would have left you alone down there, in real life?'

Dhurgham had no answer.

'You never once wrote to me,' Mr Hosni said sadly. 'Not even a postcard. No email. Nothing.'

Dhurgham's throat was dry. He couldn't speak and stared at the ceiling. Mr Hosni had the ability to sit on the bed and stay in his field of vision, however. He was older. Much older. Perhaps ill.

'The young these days are like that,' Mr Hosni said. 'No respect or love for their elders. They snip the ties,' and Mr Hosni scissored the air with his fingers. 'You are forgetting Arabic, too, the only thing that really connects you to your old parents. My daughter

Nura—not a word from her either—but I bet she's swanning it somewhere, pulling the bucks with that body.'

Dhurgham turned and looked at him in hope and horror. Mr Hosni grinned.

'Don't get high and mighty with me. She was wilful, uncontrollable. I'm not the sort to go and get her brother to shoot her for the honour of the family. I thought we all just loved each other, no questions asked. But who would be a father these days? Deserted! That's it.'

And with that Mr Hosni vanished. Dhurgham struggled to pull his father's face into his mind's eye but could only get a shoulder, an ear, a stance from a distance. He reached for his mother but she was gone. Not even her voice. His father and mother were irretrievable. He switched urgently to Nura, his memory anchor, but a half-dressed woman with a garish face intervened and laughed out loud at him. Nura was gone too. He was adrift, floating away screaming.

Who was his father anyway? Now that he couldn't recall his smell, couldn't drag his face into existence, couldn't feel or hear him, who was he? He could quote his father, but only in Dhurgham's young voice, not with any echo of the timbre of his father, a father. *The country is in the hands of a devil—A good man doesn't mix with the degraded—Who made this mess?—Your mother suffers when you are naughty, but says nothing—Feed that screeching bird—Once we cross the border, NEVER use our real name. We'll get new identity papers as soon as we get to Damascus—If we get separated, we meet together at the Great Mosque.*

He could also remember quotes and verses from the Koran but not the voice that uttered them. They had no fatherliness to them, just the cold knowledge that those now nothing lips had once held them. They had lost the mystery and glory a voice had given them. —*When Hell burns fiercely and Paradise is brought near: then each soul shall know what it has done.*

What did it add up to? Nothing. Not a person. A man. Mohammad Amer Hassan originally of Samarra. Sunni. More religious than his mother. More religious than Ahmad. A university professor. A government ... adviser. Maybe in a ministry. A political scientist, trained in London. According to Ammu, high up in a cell of the Resistance, the Opposition. Never home. Not good with children.

Father of a daughter, Nura; and Dhurgham, a son. Husband to Zahra Shammari, a Shia.

Nothing.

Mr Hosni popped his head around the closed door. He was in the middle of shaving.

'Could you check my face? I don't have a mirror,' he said, pointing at his chin and neck, and thrusting his jawbone out towards Dhurgham. 'Since you left, I've been a mess.'

• • •

He tried to talk to Carrie once. They sat together on the bench at the bottom of the garden. The grass was too wet to sit on. He turned to look at her and found he could not smile and could not tear his eyes away. He felt his eyes open up into raw holes through which she might see everything, and he couldn't twist his face into an ordinary smile or grimace, or anything to erase what he was releasing. He felt himself sucked backwards to his past, seeking his only anchor points, and still he couldn't tear his eyes away. He couldn't move. His hair rose on the back of his neck. Carrie looked at him closely.

'What?' she said, staring at his pale face. 'What?' she said more softly, shaking his arm a little. He blinked and was suddenly able to close that terrible gateway. He looked down at his hands.

'I have seen the complete beauty of the world,' he said. 'Twice. It wasn't a fleeting moment. It was burned into me, day after day. In a mosque and on an ocean. I am not sure what it means. I had to be mad or nearly dead to see it.'

Carrie looked at him, unsmiling. She didn't know what to say. She felt in that moment totally excluded; then she felt sad.

After that he told Carrie nothing. She frowned at him and went out with her friends when he was moody, leaving him to huddle in a dimmed world until she returned. Three months passed. In that time he changed. He felt himself to be walking a cliff edge between madness and hope. Nothing made any sense and he had the steady, growing awareness that his future depended on infinitely variable nothingnesses, as opaque and changeable as the clouds above this city.

Carrie's friends were going to vote for hip-hop.

'Gotya!' Mr Harwood said quietly to himself and leant back. He lit a cigarette and sighed happily. He buzzed Josie and Tulan from the other room. 'We've got him! AID's processing centre file. Listen to this: *"File Note: RRN230 A ringleader in the Easter riots 2001. Strongly influenced by POZ114, who is his self-appointed religious teacher. Confined for three days. To be monitored. No charges at this time."* "Ringleader." What a sweet word.'

'He's to be returned to custody and deported,' Mr Harwood said coldly. 'See to it.'

'On what grounds?'

'Where do I start? He escaped from processing in Australia—he broke the law.'

'We knew that in the beginning. No one's going to accept that.'

'Look, dimwit. He can face charges back there, thank God. If he goes back, we save seven billion dollars we can't do without. He's not worth one billion. Face it, Johns, he's not worth $500 000. He's not worth the time my staff have had to put into investigating him. He's bad news. He's a diplomatic disaster. He's an Iraqi, a failed, I stress *failed*, convention claimant. He has lied more times than I can count, and you still want him? Australia says he must be deported before they can talk, so he must be deported. Do it before lawyers hear of it. They won't be able to do anything once he's out of the country and buried in the Australian system.'

Mr Harwood looked him in the eye then. 'You won't miss him, Johns. Don't pretend you will. There's been talk.'

Mr Johns said nothing. What was there to say? He guessed that the grounds on which Dhurgham had failed to be given protection in Australia were technical, not substantive, or Mr Harwood would have had more to go on and would have called a press conference. But what was there to say? What was a skinny Iraqi boy next to seven billion in national interest? He felt angry with everyone, with miserable penny-pinching New Zealand, but most of all he felt unreasonably angry with Dhurgham. What a lot of trouble that boy was.

Mr Johns looked at the two on the settee. They were sitting under the large framed portrait that Dhurgham had done of Carrie. The picture disturbed him. It was very good. It showed Carrie defiant and giving, both in the one moment. It claimed a kind of knowledge and it showed something rare. It set Dhurgham apart: he could see, and create, this Carrie. The signature in Arabic was a bold, alien scrawl across her shoulder. Dhurgham had presented the framed portrait (framed, Mr Johns noted, with Carrie's money) as a gift to him and Janine a week before, and Mr Johns' predominant feeling then was that he would rather the boy had not. He had been annoyed at Janine's delight and admiration.

Dhurgham's arm was loosely over Carrie's shoulders. Carrie was sucking on a pink iceblock, staring at the TV. Two ordinary teenagers. But he could only guess at who Dhurgham might really be, might really become, and he suddenly felt unreasonably angry with Carrie too. The boy looked like a lithe, lovely young man, maybe even Maori, a local. Except for the bird of prey face—the wings of his eyebrows; and the hot, hard glance from above that Dhurgham sometimes gave. No, really, he looked like an Arab. And in the end, how could you know? Isn't it hasty to take damage into your house, expecting it to be what the surface and the face tell? Hadn't he, John Johns, been unwise to give damage some hope? He felt grim and terrible, and glad too. That arm was going to be removed and it was not his fault.

'You have to be returned to custody, I'm afraid ...' Mr Johns said slowly, trying to keep the words smooth and calm, as if what he was proposing was as minor as missing dinner.

Dhurgham turned towards him from the couch, rising from it in the same movement, uncoiling, his face flushed at first and then pale and savage. Later Janine and Carrie said that he seemed to swell, fill the room with silence, and then just … burst. Mr Johns' words, 'and deported,' were unheard.

Dhurgham felt himself rising without control but with utter precision. An instrument. His trajectory mapped out as if this was the known and practised response, a refined step in a dance that can only end one way. Then, at his uttermost, he was suddenly focused and possessed with an anger that took all painful thought and all other feeling away. In real time he erupted, froze, crashed and fell in seconds but was somehow still, frozen in that moment that was his pinnacle. Then his rage was a relief, the bursting of a great pus peak. He looked at Mr Johns, Janine and Carrie as if they were cowering together, as if they were remote. Their mouths were moving but he could only hear a roaring in his ears. He looked at them for a second with jealousy, hatred and with his head burning with the freedom to do anything to them, then he looked with pity for their innocence and their vulnerability. All this while he had not moved but was screaming, his arms outstretched, his hands like claws. He saw Carrie then as if through a mist, Carrie alone. She looked shocked and frightened, as if she were seeing a madman with no cage protecting her from him. He turned away from all three, picked up the vase of lilies and rhododendrons from the centre of the table, raised it and smashed it down through the glass top, shattering it, leaving the legs shuddering. He picked up a chair and smashed it against the frame, threw it across the room, and picked up another. The second chair left a club in his hand. Screaming and screaming. He battered the table to the floor, then smashed the club into his own head, again and again and again. He couldn't see for the screen of blood that filmed his eyeballs. He could just hear Carrie screaming with him and in some recess he felt glad that she was screaming too and he began to heave. Then he vomited as he fell unconscious into the bed of bloodied glass and crushed flowers.

'Well!' Janine said, holding Carrie close.

Carrie heard the shock in her mother's voice. She heard, dimly, that Janine was severing all ties with the form lying on the glass. She thought she should go and stroke Dhurgham's shiny hair but knew it would be bloody. She knew her mother desperately didn't want her to go. She was repulsed and ashamed of her repulsion. She struggled slightly then gave up, turning her face into her mother's chest, knowing what her mother's response would be. Janine tightened her grip and turned her daughter's face and body away, as if they had just witnessed a stranger fall from a great height to the pavement in front of them.

Mr Johns called the ambulance. He was relieved to see the unconscious form of the boy blanketed in white and driven away. The paramedic said he thought the boy had fainted, nothing more. The cuts were superficial. But Mr Johns saw the despair. He knew that Dhurgham had just lost more than freedom. Mr Johns felt like a traitor, old and shifty. He saw himself as if from the outside and pushed away the idea that he had not fought much for Dhurgham this time, that he had just let things happen because he wanted to retrieve his daughter. It was only a moment. Carrie comes first, he told himself. He wanted that volcanic pain as far from his family as possible.

'Well!' Janine said again.

Dhurgham hurt all over. He lay in the yellow light of the prison cell, probing his confusion, pain and rage for something. He didn't want Carrie. He had dimly seen her face as he broke the Johns' furniture and he had smashed harder when he felt himself smashing their love. Yes, he saw in her eyes that he was not human. His heart stilled. Not Human. Mr Hosni had called him an Angel. And Birdie. The winged boy. Shaitan. Monster.

He wanted Nura.

To have no easy space against the skin and limbs of another, to have no known sister body, itself linked to all the rest of the world! That was worse than being an orphan, worse than having the lover turn her face from you in horror. He fought a rising fear that he was really not human; not male, not female. He lay in the dark and fingered his belly button, feeling for his babyhood, his birth, remembering Nura. He bedded his memory with her. He found her body suddenly with unbearable clarity. It was Nura (rarely his mother, never his father) who had cuddled him, always had her hands on him. Feeling back into memory, he knew his own child thigh pressed against hers, his child spine clasped tight between her ribs and knees, his ear pressed to hers, listening for the mysteries of the sea in her ear shell. He had had her once, his older sister, his trailblazer, his scout, his link into life.

He held up his cut and scratched hands against the cream brick wall. He noticed that the beautiful watch was broken. The glass was gone and the hands were grotesque and motionless, twisted up off the face like the antennae of an alert insect.

He began to weep.

Dominion Post

NZ HOODWINKED BY CRIM— ASSAMARRAI NO REFUGEE

Thurgam Assamarrai, the Iraqi convention claimant from Australia, is to be deported, whether he likes it or not.

Mr Assamarrai will be returned to Australia to face charges for various crimes, including damage to property and inciting to violence.

He has been described by AID Australia as a 'ringleader' in riots in 2001 in which more than a million dollars worth of damage was done to government property at Mawirrigun Aliens Processing Centre.

'These people can't just decide they don't like Australia after all and give New Zealand a try,' Ted Harwood, Deputy to the Minister for Immigration said today.

Mr Assamarrai, aged 18, made a failed bid for refugee status in Australia after arriving illegally in 1999. He then escaped from the Kanugo Kagil APC in Sydney last December and attempted to sneak into New Zealand in the stowage of a luxury yacht. Once apprehended, in a bizarre twist, he claimed persecution by Australia under the 1951 Convention to which New Zealand is a signatory.

'New Zealand has been a bit naive with its touchy-feely approach to illegals,' the Australian Immigration Minister Ross Cowell said today. 'It has now made itself into a target for these people.'

Mr Assamarrai will be returned to custody in Australia, although where, the minister would not say. He will be placed under maximum security, following his escape.

'Processing is as pleasant a place as we can make it,' Minister Cowell said, 'but if you break the rules, we are left with few options.'

When asked whether Mr Assamarrai would be incarcerated in an ordinary prison, the Minister said, 'That remains to be seen. He has been involved in a number of criminal activities in Australia, beginning with entering illegally.'

Minister Cowell has direct responsibility, in his capacity as Protector of Aliens, for Mr Assamarrai's wellbeing. It is not a guardianship he takes lightly, he assured the Dominion Post today.

Mr Assamarrai is among a number of failed convention claimants awaiting deportation to their countries of origin. However, as Iraq has no arrangement with Australia to accept deportees, Mr Assamarrai must wait. For how long? Until Minister Cowell finds someone who will have him.

It could be a long wait.

Dhurgham awoke with a terrible headache. He was in a tiny plane which was banking steeply over a strange land. He had been slumped sideways, with saliva running from the corner of his mouth onto his T-shirt. His temples throbbed and he was very cold. There was one other person there, seated directly across the toy-sized aisle from him. An AID official, judging by the uniform. The plane dropped and glided over some shabby sheds with *Towilla Marsh Air Base* in white letters painted on the tin roof, then skimmed just above tall reeds and golden grasses in a bare wet land.

At the steps of the plane he was still in a daze. The three men waiting looked like Australian police and AID. They all had pistols. One of the police officers stepped forward and Dhurgham noticed dimly that he had that familiar alertness of the very new. He reached for Dhurgham's limp hand, turning and talking to the Australian guard as he tried to flick a handcuff onto Dhurgham's wrist. It slid off the first time, then gripped.

The clicking sound and the metal against Dhurgham's skin galvanised him. Before anyone could register what was happening, he was away, ducking under the still-whining wing of the airplane, just missing the deadly shadow of the prop, then trotting fast over the dilapidated tarmac and towards the golden sedge and reeds. The brief blast of wind from the whirring blade had fully woken him. The flurry and frantic shouts the other side of the propeller barely touched him. The wet land stretched away before him as far as he could see, scattered with fragments of white plastic bags and other desiccated rubbish caught in grass stalks. Irregular sheets of water glittered silver between the grasses. He was at the edge of the bitumen in seconds and strode out. A marsh smell rose to his nostrils as the spongy ground gave beneath his feet. A lone bird hovered, moving and motionless, so near that he could see its clear eye and steady, detached regard. It was a peregrine—so familiar! Other, smaller birds rose into the sky with a faint whirring sound. The empty seed heads on golden stalks sang in the wind and he felt his body thrumming with something altogether unexpected.

Distantly he heard a voice calling him to stop and the sound of pounding feet on asphalt. He trotted on without turning.

He suddenly saw Mr Hosni, body bowed over that familiar kitchen table, silently weeping. Mr Hosni's mother was stroking her son's sparse hair with long gentle strokes, her face still and calm. Dhurgham saw again, as if he were in that room, the old woman's hand and its loving stroke. It was a wrinkled, heavy hand with thickened hooked nails, stern with grief. He hovered with that hand, almost felt it himself, as fatherloss welled up into the world around him. He saw Mr Hosni's unassuagable pain and the frailty of a beloved but castaway son's shoulders. And he saw again but without envy how terrible and precious it was to be loved. He saw Mr Hosni as if from far away, yet right there in his heart, with his own hand settling inside that old woman's. He felt himself touch the remote world that was Mr Hosni's head, not to hold, not to belong, not to ask or beg. A lightest touch before take-off.

A hard grip on his heart opened and something flew away with the rising birds, leaving him in bliss. Of course! Mr Hosni had returned. First it had to be Mr Hosni.

'I am the dot!' he said.

He passed Mr Hosni and looked to the ground at his spattering feet. The marshes were clear and limpid ahead, their fresh wet smell rising in his nostrils. He squinted into the light, seeking that darkness.

A shot was fired into the air and all the marsh birds rose with a sudden uprush and the whistle and percussion of beating wings. He was running hard now, in long skimming strides, his heart as full and as empty as the sky.

He felt a sharp pain in his chest and felt himself lift with the birds; and then he was in that other darkened, deeper marsh, glinting in unrevealed starlight, not the morning sun. *I am the dot!* he sang without words.

He thought he saw Nura's hijab, gleaming white just ahead. Beyond her, maybe, the distant white sails of the *Morning Star* gliding in the stillness of a mosaic. Then he heard his mother's voice, clear and close. He felt her breath on his neck, her kiss on his earlobe: *Be the first! Run, Dhurgham darling, run!*

And, completely happy, he ran.

ACKNOWLEDGMENTS

A special acknowledgment and thanks to Nuha al Radi for her time, her vibrant correspondence, and her intense, honest, critical warmth towards my writing. Her death on 31 August 2004 is a huge loss. A much needed voice is now silent.

Many people contributed in different ways to this book. They are: Amal Abou-Hamden, Fayrouz Ajaka, Annette Barlow, Deslie Billich, Vivian Bradley, Neil Brown, Nyssa Brown, Julian Burnside, Juan Cole, Rose Creswell, Mary Crock, Azadeh Dastyari, Sonja Dechian, Adeeb Kamal ad-Deen, Jenni Devereaux, Abbas El-Zein, Raimond Gaita, Hamida, Hawraa

Hamami, Mariana Hardwick, Winton Higgins, L'hibou Hornung, Sue Hosking, Annette Hughes, Linda Jaivin, Raed Jarrar, Joe Laino, Gina Lennox, Alan Lindsay, Tom Mann, Peter Mares, Sarah Margan, Lesley McFadzean, Don McMaster, Tim Materne, Khalid Melhi, Heather Millar, Ann Mitcalfe, Kate Mitcalfe, Alex Mitcalfe Wilson, Gavin Mooney, Jeremy Moore, Gaylene Morgan, Christa Munns, Walid Mutawakkil, Raghid Nahhas, Mohamed Moustafa Nassar, Abdallah Osman, Salam Pax, Lindy Powell, Cathy Preston-Thomas, Nuha al Radi, Riverbend, Meki al Saegh, Muneera Sallis, Roger Sallis, Yahia As-Samawi, Arwa Shamhan, Tom Shapcott, Jack Smit, Sandy Thorne, Heather Tyler, Philip Waldron, Rod Wells, Teresita White.

A special thanks to Dr Raghid Nahhas, editor of *Kalimat*, for field research in Damascus and for much thoughtful advice.

Australian and international government departments, companies, NGOs and other community organisations, groups and projects provided invaluable source materials, including detailed reports and commentaries. These organisations, groups and projects include: Ausnews Global Network, Australian Education Union, Australian Refugees Association, Australians Against Racism Inc, Australia IS Refugees! Schools Competition 2002 and There is No Place Like Home 2004, the Catholic Commission for Justice Development and Peace, Children Out of Detention

(ChilOut), Department of Immigration Multicultural and Indigenous Affairs (DIMIA), Human Rights and Equal Opportunity Commission, Human Rights Watch, Project Safecom, Refugee Advocacy Service South Australia (RASSA), Refugee Council of Australia, Refugee Review Tribunal (RRT), Rural Australians for Refugees (RAR), Salt Writers, Seeking Asylum Alone, SIEVX.com, United Nations Association Australia, UNHCR, Victoria Chambers, and Vue Pty Ltd. Finally, a number of asylum seekers' court proceedings provided important and valuable source materials.

Mawirrigun is a fictional detention centre; so is Kanugo Kagil. AID is a fictional government ministry, as are other departments, tribunals or organisations mentioned in this book. All are the creative product of research. The Hope Caravan and Freedom Bus are real.

Hassan Ajmi is a real café on al Mutanabbi Street in Baghdad but the description of it is entirely fictional.

Uncle Mahmoud in hospital is loosely based on the description of embargo conditions in Nuha al Radi's *Baghdad Diaries* (Saqi 1998).

The three rude little girls and the conflict over washing vessels episodes are loosely based on events described in Sandy Thorne's *Beyond the Razorwire … is Australia, where everything's Free.*

Aziz's story is loosely based on that of Nasir Khadi Hazim al Husseini, a twelve-year-old survivor of a mass execution. 'The Mass Graves of al Mahawil: The Truth Uncovered: VIII A Survivor' Human Rights Watch Report 2003.

Dhurgham's drawings are inspired by those of Meki al Saegh, an artist who was detained in Woomera in 2000, now living in Iran.

Abu Nizar's CV is loosely based on that of Mohamed Moustafa Nassar, used with his permission.

Thank you to the SA Writers' Centre for my Wednesday office in 2003.

Quotes from the Koran are from The Thunder (Surat al Ra'd), The Cessation (Surat al Takwir), and The Merciful (Surat al Rahman).

Finally, I owe a huge thank you to the Australia Council Literature Fund. Two grants made this book possible, one awarded in 2000 (principally given for *Mahjar*) and another in 2003.

ALSO FROM ALLEN & UNWIN

Fire Fire
Eva Sallis

'Musicians, artists and poets,' Acantia says. 'That's what you'll be. Just like Pa and me.' She sighs happily. 'No contaminants here! You'll be as pure as the Aborigines.'

The Houdinis have escaped the great world to Whispers, a dilapidated and isolated farm in the heart of the Australian bush. Acantia Houdini the painter has grand plans. Her seven children and famous violist husband are to become self-sufficient, and creativity will rule.

All is not, however, home-grown spinach and classical music. The family is under threat from the outside and from within.

Ursula watches her brothers and sisters adapt, thrive and then wither as they experience a bewildering mix of love, neglect and cruelty. Ursula grows slowly to a full awareness of her skewed world and is driven ultimately to escape. But it will cost her more than she can guess. Family is everything. She has everything to lose.

Fire Fire is shocking, absurd, tender and grotesque. In language spun with masterly control and much humour, Sallis captures the resilience and confusion of growing up.

'Slashed with its multiple flashes of refining fire and humour both subtle and ribald, Fire Fire is a dark and powerful fable.' Katherine England, Adelaide Advertiser

ISBN 1 74114 352 7